HARVEST AMERICAN
Writing

Trying to Smile

and Other Stories

SARA LEWIS

Trying to Smile
and Other Stories

A HARVEST BOOK

HARCOURT BRACE & COMPANY

San Diego • New York • London

Requests for permission to make copies of any part of
the work should be mailed to: Permissions Department,
Harcourt Brace & Company, 6277 Sea Harbor Drive,
Orlando, Florida 32887-6777.

"Perfect Combinations," "One Whole Day," and
"The First Weekend" originally appeared in the *New Yorker*;
"Trouble People" originally appeared in *Seventeen*, May 1986;
"Trying to Smile" originally appeared
in the *Mississippi Review*, Vol. 14, No. 3, 1986;
"As P.T." originally appeared
in the *Mississippi Review*, Vol. 17, No. 3, 1989;
and "Celia" originally appeared in *Redbook*
under the title "Mothers Make Mistakes."

Library of Congress Cataloging-in-Publication Data
Lewis, Sara,
Trying to smile and other stories/Sara Lewis.—1st ed.
p.   cm.
Contents: Gone—Perfect combinations—One whole
day—Trouble people—Trying to smile—The first weekend—
As P.T.—ESP experiments—Celia
ISBN 0-15-191312-9   ISBN 0-15-600395-3 (pbk.)
I. Title.
PS3562.E9745T78   1992
813'.54—dc20   91-42468

Type set in Goudy Old Style
Designed by Camilla Filancia
Printed in the United States of America
First Harvest edition 1996   A B C D E

For Kees

Contents

I am grateful to a number of people for helping this book come about. Melinda A. Knight of New York University is responsible for getting me started. She gave me encouragement, support, and a lot of her time. Edie Soderberg read many drafts of all the stories in this book with endless enthusiasm and patience. I also counted on my sister, Susannah Lewis, for intelligent reading and comments, which she gave generously. Editors Mary D. Kierstead of the *New Yorker*, Rie Fortenberry of the *Mississippi Review*, Bonni Price of *Seventeen*, Eileen Schnurr of *Mademoiselle*, and Dawn Raffel of *Redbook* helped enormously by buying my stories. Their work on the stories themselves, as well as that of Claire Wachtel and Ruth Greenstein of Harcourt Brace Jovanovich, was significant and valuable. Finally, I thank my agent, Robert Colgan, for his wit and kindness and for always handling everything perfectly.

Trying to Smile

and Other Stories

Gone

I was in my parents' bathroom braiding the wig my mother was wearing, trying to make her look like a hippie. It was Halloween, 1970. I was sixteen. Two strands of each braid were wig hair, and the third was purple ribbon. I was going to do nine of these, three on each side and three in the back, but my mother wouldn't hold still. "Don't laugh," I said. "It's getting late, and I've only got one side done." My brother Charles, who was twelve, was sitting on the edge of the bath-tub. He shook his head at our mother and covered his face with his hands. Lily, who was eight, was sitting on the lid of the toilet in her ballerina costume. This was Lily's third year as a ballerina. She took ballet lessons every Saturday, but Halloween was her only chance to wear a pink tutu and slippers that laced up the ankles, not to mention lipstick. She kept peeking around the bathroom door, as if she heard someone —our father—coming. But he was out of town at a scientific conference in Arizona. If he had been around, our mother would not be dressed as a hippie, even on Halloween. Our mother had a goofy streak a mile wide, something she tried to keep in check when our father was around.

"All right," Mom said. "Let's be very serious now." She didn't laugh again until I was putting the rubber band around my final ribbon braid. She was taking Lily and some friends trick-or-treating as soon as it got dark. Charles and I, who were both past trick-or-treating, would stay home and hand out candy to the kids who came to our house. The idea for the costume had started downtown this afternoon in Thrifty, where our mother was buying Scotch tape and cotton balls. As she was heading for the checkout counter with the three of us following her, she saw a long auburn wig with bangs on sale for five dollars. "Look, Cathy," she said to me. "What do you think?" and she put it on. A little fringe of her real hair—brown and parted on the side, held back with two crisscrossed bobby pins—hung out from under the glossy synthetic mane. She found a mirror on a carousel of sunglasses and laughed so hard at herself that she had to bend over and rest her hands on her knees.

I said, "Yeah. Buy it, Mom."

Lily said, "Don't. Take it off." She looked behind her to see if other customers were watching, but there was no one around. She reached up and tried to grab the wig. But Mom was too fast for Lily, ducking away, then putting a hand on her hip and striking a vampish pose.

"That is so ugly," Charles said. "Get it, Mom. I dare you."

"I'm going to," she said. She looked in the mirror and laughed again. The ribbon and braids were my idea.

By the time we got home, it was already four. My mother and I rummaged around in my closet—making a big mess because we were in such a hurry—until we found an old pair of my jeans. Two years before, in ninth grade, I had patched them all over in different kinds of material—blue paisley on the knees, green corduroy on the rear end, and red velvet around the cuffs. She couldn't button them, but that was all right, because on top she wore a baggy old work shirt of my father's that hung over the jeans. She borrowed my sandals and put a little silver ring around one of her toes.

Lily said, "I don't think the other mothers are dressing up, Mom." The same things that made Charles and me laugh at our mother made Lily nervous and embarrassed.

"Yes, they are," our mother said. "Joanna's mother is going as a witch, and Laurie's mother is going as a vampire or a Martian—I forget what she said." Lily chewed at a hangnail.

I tied a purple scarf around my mother's forehead. "Good," I said, admiring my work. "She looks funny, Lil," I said. "People will laugh."

"Oh," Lily said. "Dad wouldn't like it, I bet."

"But Dad's not here, Lil," said Charles. "Relax, would you?"

Our father, a physics professor at the university, was in a terrible mood these days. Recently the students had boycotted classes to protest the war in Vietnam and spray-painted antigovernment slogans and cartoons of President Nixon all over the building where his lab was. Other professors his age were growing their hair and sideburns long, as if they were members of middle-aged rock bands. Secretaries and graduate students addressed him by his first name. Our father was irritated all the time. He liked things the way they were before. He had voted for Nixon twice.

Now our father shouted at us every night at the dinner table, his face turning dark red with fury. We did everything wrong. One night he made Lily shake hands with him over and over (she cried the whole time) until he was convinced that everyone she met for the rest of her life would know from her firm grasp that she came from a good family. Charles had to stand in the backyard for an hour once, throwing a ball overhand, while our father stood on the patio and yelled,

"Use your goddamn legs!" I did more wrong than anyone. My voice was nasal, he said, my hair was too long, and my math skills were appalling. Sometimes I set him off on purpose. I worked the word "irrelevant" into the conversation, knowing it would trigger an explosive speech on overused words. I refused to eat meat, saying no one could prove that animals did not have souls. I preferred his chasing me, yelling about insolence, out into the driveway to his shouting at the others, especially Mom. She tried too hard and crumpled when our father got mad at her.

Almost every day, she had some little surprise to cheer him up—a gadget she had sent away for to give him as a present, a fancy dessert, a joke she had heard, a new book that supported his views exactly. She tried to foresee the things that would annoy him and correct them before they happened. Every evening, she checked our rooms to make sure they were tidy. She reorganized the refrigerator and cupboards to use space more economically. And she read two newspapers daily while we were at school, in case our father wanted to discuss anything. I was her assistant, her deputy. "No job too small, no job too large," I would say, as I called from downtown to tell her that I had found saffron for the soup she was making or as I ironed a king-sized flat sheet.

"O.K., you guys," said our mother, "I'm ready." She made a peace sign at us, two fingers in a V. "Lily, go get your shoes on or we're going to be late."

I was in the kitchen dumping a bag of miniature candy bars into a salad bowl when I heard a car in the driveway. I rushed to find my monster mask and wig and then hurried to the front hall with the bowl. Charles was painting gory wounds and black stitches on his face, using the hall mirror. Our mother padded down the hall, the sandals flapping against her heels. "Anyone seen my keys?" she said. Lily was behind her, fluffing out the skirt of her tutu.

The front door opened before I reached it. Our father walked in with his briefcase full of journals in one hand and his suitcase in the other. "Dad," I said. "Happy Halloween."

Our mother said, "You're back early. How was the meeting?"

He stared at her. He looked at the wig, at the jeans, at the shoes, then closed the door behind him.

"Hi, Dad," Lily said, in a hoarse whisper. "I'm a ballerina. Again."

Our father glanced at us, pressed his lips together, and went through the kitchen out to the patio.

We heard a chair scrape against the concrete outside. Our mother whispered to me, "Get the meatloaf out of the refrigerator and put it in the oven. Put on three cups of water for rice, and start washing some lettuce. Got that?" I nodded. "Thanks, punkin. Lily, you go with Joanna and Laurie. I have to stay here."

Lily's face clouded up as she tried not to cry.

"I'll go with you," Charles said. "Come on, where's your candy bag?"

"Thank you, Charles," our mother said. She walked on her toes to the stairs to keep the sandals from flapping. "Cathy, I'll be right down." Halfway up the steps, she pulled off the wig and tossed it down to me. I caught it and took it to the kitchen, where I stuffed it in the cupboard behind some paper bags.

In the morning, my best friend, Denise, picked me up for school. Denise had bought a car as soon as she got her driver's license the year before. It was a '61 Ford station wagon. It was brown and cost two hundred dollars. I spent a lot of time with Denise. It wasn't tense at her house the way it was at ours. Denise's father hadn't lived with them since she was little, and her mother was pretty relaxed.

In the front seat, I slid way down and started to take off my clothes. First I took off my white cardigan, folded it, and put it on the seat next to me. I also took off my gray jumper but left on the blue turtleneck I was wearing underneath. From a paper bag down by my feet, I pulled out a white sailor shirt I had bought at the Army-Navy store. It was a real one that some actual Navy guy had worn. Whenever I had it on, men my father's age came up to me to explain what the little symbols sewn on the sleeves meant. It was big, so I rolled the cuffs up. Then I put on a pair of Levi's that I had washed many times over at Denise's until they were soft. (At home, not only were we not allowed to wear jeans, but my dad would never have permitted washing anything that wasn't truly dirty.) My jeans were starting to wear thin on one knee, and I was looking forward to the rip that would soon appear there, letting my knee stick out between frayed threads. I took off my penny loafers, barely scuffed on the bottom, and put on a pair of brown-and-white saddle shoes I had bought at the Salvation Army for thirty-five cents.

Denise said, "Feel better?"

I said, "Yes, thank you."

That day was way too hot for November first, even for California. For the seventh time in a row, the temperature was in the high eighties. Up in the hills a few miles away, a fire had been burning in the dry grass since around midnight. I kept wearing the wrong clothes to school, expecting it to cool off.

Our first class was American Government. Because of the heat, Mrs. Garabedian had us sit outside. This didn't help, because out on the lawn behind the library there was no shade.

"I'm getting sunstroke," I whispered to Denise. Then I saw something that confirmed it. My mother was walking across the grass, wearing sunglasses and the old plaid shorts she used for gardening. There was dirt on her knees. She walked up to Mrs. Garabedian and spoke to her in a low voice. I sat up. The teacher said, "Cathy, you're excused for today." Everyone turned around to look at me.

"What?" I said. "I mean, I need a pass, don't I?" For some reason, I didn't want to go with my mother; I wanted to stay right here.

"No pass," Mrs. Garabedian said. "Go, sweetheart. I'll take care of it."

I felt cool suddenly as the blood drained away from my face and my hands became clammy. No teacher had ever called me sweetheart. I picked up my books and followed Mom to the car. Lily was in front and Charles in back, their pale, anxious faces peering out at us through the open windows.

I got in next to Charles. Our mother sat behind the wheel and put the key in the ignition. She turned so that we could all see her and took her sunglasses off. Her eyes were red. "Children," she said, "your father is gone." The last word didn't come out right. It was a short, pinched squeak at the end of the sentence, and I thought, Divorce. But that wasn't it. Our mother was making a little speech that included the words *hospital, massive coronary, loved you all very much*. It took me a moment to realize that by "gone" she didn't mean just away, but *dead*. The air was sucked out of the car, and everything looked dark. I put my head back on the seat.

Charles and Lily started crying, and there weren't any Kleenex. I dug around in my purse and found some napkins from Taco Bell. I handed one to Charles, one to Lily, and one to our mother. I was not crying. I just had this problem about breathing. I felt desperate for oxygen, but as soon as I started to inhale, I found that my lungs were already full of too much air.

A few minutes later, our mother started the car and headed home, holding her soggy napkin against the steering wheel. I had a feeling that the world was about to spin loose, that a natural law had suddenly proven false. When we got to our road, we saw Mrs. Riemer standing in front of her house. She was clipping her hedge, wearing a big straw hat and white cream on her nose. As our car passed, she waved and went on clipping. I wanted to roll down my window and yell, "Don't you *know*? Can't you see? Our father died. You can't just *wave* at us."

In the house, our mother said, "Listen, now. People are going to call and come over to offer their condolences. They're going to say, 'I'm sorry about your father.' Do you know what you're supposed to say back? You say 'Thank you.' All right? They say they're sorry, you thank them."

We all said, "O.K."

Our mother was on the phone the rest of the morning, telling the story exactly the same way to everybody. She said that last night after dinner our father went back to the university to work on something he and Professor Minnikel had going at the lab. He left the house early this morning, just the way he always did, and the next thing she knew—she was weeding out front—Dr. Martinez was calling from intensive care. By the time she got down to the hospital, Alan (our father) was gone. She always said "gone," instead of "dead." Sometimes she put her hand over her eyes, as if shielding them from a bright light, and tried to make her voice sound even. She told about the medicine for high blood pressure that our father never took, the diet he didn't follow, and the stress-reducing exercise program he kept postponing. She ended by saying that the funeral would be Friday.

In the afternoon, our neighbor Mrs. Riemer walked down our driveway. She had wiped the cream off her nose and removed her sun hat. She was carrying a casserole dish, and balanced on top of it was something in a paper bag. Under her arm was a bunch of gardenias from her garden wrapped in a cone of newspaper. "I heard," she said to our mother. She looked at the three of us. "I'm so sorry."

There was a little pause, then we all said, "Thank you."

Mrs. Riemer handed the casserole dish to our mother. "You can freeze this, or heat it up tonight, whatever."

"Thank you very much," said our mother. "How nice."

"And this is for all of you." She handed the bag to me.

Inside was a puzzle. Fifteen hundred pieces, the box said. The picture was a medieval painting of the Tower of Babel. I said, "Thank you," again.

Mrs. Riemer said, "Now, don't feel you have to like it. Just do it if you want to or throw it away if you don't, or leave it on a shelf for a year—whatever. This is no time to be polite. How *are* you kids?" Mrs. Riemer wrinkled her brow, to let us know she cared about our answer.

"Fine," we all said.

"Well, of course you are. Yes." She handed the gardenias to our mother.

"These smell just wonderful, don't they, kids?" our mother said. We all nodded.

Mrs. Riemer said, "Is there *anything* I can do?" My mother shook her head. "Well, if you think of something, please call me. Even if it's just to talk, pick up that phone. In the middle of the night, whenever. Or don't call. Whatever you need to do." She reached out to Mom, who put the casserole on a chair. Mrs. Riemer took hold of both her hands and squeezed. My mother's eyes filled up again, and Mrs. Riemer hugged her. She clung to the back of our neighbor's blouse for a long time. It looked odd to me to see her hugging the woman who lived down the street. Mrs. Riemer shut her eyes and bit her bottom lip. When my mother let go and backed a few steps away, wiping her eyes, Mrs. Riemer turned to leave. The back of her blouse was wrinkled in the two places Mom had held on to. At the front door, she said to us, "I'll be around. You call me. I mean it."

Two secretaries from the physics department and one of my father's graduate students came by, bringing a big flower arrangement with a card from my father's lab. The graduate student, Quentin, sat next to me on the couch and pulled at his cuticles. A secretary named Annabelle with hair to her waist and earrings to her shoulders said to us, "We're all real sorry about, you know, what happened to your dad."

The other woman, Debbie, nodded and said, "Yeah, really."

Charles said, "Thank you," and his nostrils flared.

I poked a fingernail under the cellophane of Mrs. Riemer's puzzle and took the top off the box. For a second, I was stunned by the number and small size of the pieces. We'll never finish this, I thought. Quentin looked over my shoulder at the picture on the lid of the box and said, "Cool puzzle."

I said, "Thank you."

When they left, our mother put the flowers from the lab on the mantel and Mrs. Riemer's gardenias on the coffee table. I took a lamp, an ashtray, and two magazines off a table in the corner and pulled up some chairs. Then I sat down and started to spread out the puzzle pieces. Lily and Charles sat down with me. I said, "Get all the sky pieces and put them over here. And this is going to be a pile for the pieces with these little brick things. See those lines, Lily? Here, look at the picture. That's this part. When you find one of those, put it here, O.K.?"

Charles bent low to the table and started a new pile with the first two pieces he picked up. He pointed to them. "Edge pieces, you guys."

The house began to smell like gardenias.

In a dressing room on the third floor of Bullock's, my mother and I were sitting in our underwear, waiting for the saleswoman to come back with more dresses for us to try on. So far, we had each tried one that we didn't like. That morning my mother had surveyed all the closets for funeral clothes. She found a navy-blue jumper and white blouse for Lily, and for Charles she got out a blue blazer and gray flannel pants. I didn't have anything suitable, she said, and she didn't like any of her own clothes, either. Our grandparents, Fred and Nonny, who had arrived from Chicago the night before, were at home with Lily and Charles. They were our mother's parents. Our father's mother had died before I was born and his father died when I was little.

"I was going to have a garage sale," my mother was saying now, staring at some straight pins on the carpet. The elastic of her bra was worn; her breasts drooped. "I wanted to get rid of all the junk we've accumulated. And I meant to get some pictures framed of you kids." Eyeing herself in the mirror, she pulled at her hair. The perm was almost grown out, so that it was flat on top and not curly anymore but just a little frizzy at the ends. She took out her bobby pins and put them in again. "I was going to get my hair done weeks ago and never got around to that, either."

"Maybe you can still make an appointment for this afternoon," I said.

"Oh, I could," said my mother. "It's just that I meant to do all these things—I mean—you know what I mean."

She meant that she had a few more things she wanted to try that she thought might snap Dad into a better mood, like a switch turning on a light. I said, "I think your hair looks pretty. I do."

My mother looked at the dressing-room curtain and said, "She's been away a long time. I hope she doesn't think we're going to spend a lot of money."

When the saleswoman came back, she had three more dresses for each of us. "Here we are, ladies," she said. She hung them on two hooks and left us again. Immediately I saw the dress I wanted and took it off the hanger. It was a black knit minidress with a high neck of loosely gathered folds of material. The sleeves were a little long, also bunching at the wrists. There were three round buttons in the back and two each on the cuffs. I put it on. It fit. "I'll take this one," I said.

"Fine," my mother said without even looking or asking the price. I did up the dress she was trying. She glanced at herself briefly. "I'll take this one, too. Unzip me, would you? I want to get out of this tiny room and away from that mirror."

The morning of the funeral, we rode to the church in a limousine. My mother, Grandpa Fred, Nonny, and I sat on the wide back seat; Charles and Lily sat on jump seats. My mother's sister Betty and her husband Mike followed in a rented Buick. They had gotten here from Illinois the night before. My grandfather pushed a button to lower the back window a crack and let out the smoke from his cigarette but not the air-conditioning. A strong, warm wind, a Santa Ana, had blown all night. A small tree was down in our front yard. The wind was fanning new fires in the hills, which were eating up an increasing number of acres. It was too hot for the dress I had chosen and the tights I was wearing with it, but it would only be for a couple of hours.

A man from the church was waiting for us when the limousine pulled up. He led us inside. We had only been here a few times. We had to wait on a bench in a side room in the church, while slow organ music played inside. Charles got fidgety and rolled his tie up from the bottom, let it unroll, then rolled it up again. Grandpa Fred put his hand on Charles's arm, and he stopped rolling. Lily leaned her head against our mother's arm. Then the man opened a door and beckoned us inside. Lily went first, then Charles, me, our mother, Aunt Betty, and Uncle Mike. The front row was roped off for us with one of those velvety red things used for bank lines. The man unhooked this and we all filed in and sat down.

The church was dark and cool. Candles were burning on the altar next to two flower arrangements on either side of a big cross. A few rows behind us, a woman coughed. I wanted to see who had come, but I didn't think I should turn around. The minister walked in silently from a door on the left that I couldn't see. He told us what page to turn to in the hymnal. A few times during the hymn, my voice wandered way off the tune, which was too high for me. I decided to just move my lips as if I were singing, in case I was throwing anyone else off. When we sat down again, the minister read from the Bible, then gave a little speech about my father. "Alan Phipps, cherished husband, beloved father," he began, which sounded strange to me, as if I were hearing about someone I had never met.

When the service was over, I followed my family down the aisle and out the front door of the church. A little crowd formed at the top of the church steps as people came out. Hair, skirts, and the backs of suit jackets flapped wildly in the wind. I stood next to my mother, who was shaking hands with each person and saying, "Thank you for coming," over and over again. Fred and Nonny stood on the other side of her. Aunt Betty and Uncle Mike waited with Charles and Lily in the shade of a big fig tree.

My friend Denise had gotten out of school to come to the funeral with her mother, Charlotte, who was wearing a black hat with a wide brim. First Denise hugged me. She didn't say anything. We weren't used to hugging each other, and it felt awkward. Then Charlotte hugged me.

"Neat hat," I said. She was holding it with one hand to keep it from blowing away.

"Oh, honey," Charlotte said softly, "next time you come over, I'll give it to you."

"Are you coming to our house now?" I said.

"We can't," Charlotte said. "Denise has a geometry test." Denise rolled her eyes.

"Oh," I said, "see you."

"See you," said Denise.

A young woman came out of the church blowing her nose on a white handkerchief and walked over to me. She was pretty, with big blue eyes and blond hair to her shoulders, probably a student. I put my hand out, and the woman took it in both of hers and held it, looking into my eyes. We were wearing the same dress. I was going to say something about this, but the woman spoke first. "You must be Cathy," she said. "I'm Myrna Minnikel." I opened my mouth but didn't say anything. "Professor Minnikel from your father's department?" A strand of blond hair blew across her face and stuck to her lip gloss. She said, "Your father and I were very close." Her eyes filled with tears. "He meant the world to me."

"Oh," I said. I looked at my mother, who was talking to Mrs. Riemer about what a godsend the puzzle was. "Mom?" I said.

Mrs. Riemer hugged her and said, "You're stronger than you think, dear." Then she went down the steps.

It was Professor Minnikel's turn to talk to my mother. In a quiet, soft voice, she said, "We loved a wonderful man," and leaned forward to kiss my mother on the cheek.

My mother drew her head back and made a face, as if she had just smelled something foul. "What are you doing here?" she said. Professor Minnikel held up her hands and tried to speak. "Go away!" my mother said. People who were already walking to their cars turned around. "Go. Now. Get away!" she said, her voice going up as high as a child's. Then she gave Professor Minnikel a push. Professor Minnikel grabbed a banister, but my mother lost her balance and stumbled down three steps. The wind lifted the hem of her dress in back so that, for a second, you could see her legs all the way to the top where her varicose veins were so bad. My grandfather caught her arm to keep her from falling. Professor Minnikel said, "I'm sorry I upset you," and walked down the church steps to the sidewalk.

For a second after she had left, there was a sluggish, dull feeling in my brain as if it were stuffed with cotton and couldn't make way for this new information. My mother's lower lip quivered uncontrollably as she shook the rest of the hands. I pushed rudely past Professor Elkin and his overweight wife without saying hello or excuse me. My father would have yelled at me for that, but he was dead. I went to the limousine. The chauffeur was leaning on the front of it, smoking. I stood by the back door and waited until he saw me and rushed around to open it. "Thank you," I said, climbing in like a member of some deposed royal family.

In the car, I forced myself to imagine my father kissing Professor Minnikel on the mouth, his fingers all over her face. I thought about all the silly schemes I had helped my mother with, trying to pull him out of his unhappiness. What he was so mad about lately had nothing to do with throwing a ball, handshakes, or math. It had nothing to do with student unrest, either. What made him so furious was us, ourselves, and the fact that we were not Professor Minnikel.

When we got home, there were cars parked in our driveway and down the street. It was like a party, I thought, only everyone wore dark clothes and spoke softly and there was no music. The guests didn't stay long, either. After about an hour, everyone had cleared out. Nonny and Aunt Betty collected all the dirty glasses on a tray and took them to the kitchen. Uncle Mike vacuumed up all the leaves and dust that had blown in every time the front door opened. My grandfather told Lily and Charles a story about a pony that bit him when he was little. Then it was time for them all to go to the airport for their plane home.

When they had left, I got Charles and Lily going on the puzzle, then went to my mother's room. She was lying on her side of the bed, still in her black dress, with one arm over her eyes. She didn't move when I came in. "I suppose you want to know how long it was going on," she said. "Two years. Everything was fine before then. We had a nice, happy family. Remember our treasure hunts? We had such a good time when we all went to Yosemite. Then the damn hippies came along and suddenly black was white and the truth a lie."

"Hippies?" I said. "She didn't look like a hippie to me. And Dad was practically a redneck."

"You know what I mean." She sat up and waved her hands

around. "It was in the air. Nothing was good enough anymore. He said the two of them read Fitzgerald stories aloud to each other. Your father didn't read fiction. Ever. And I knew him almost twenty years." My mother's eyes narrowed. "She has a motorcycle. He bought her a helmet."

I said, "Mom, everyone was miserable. He yelled at us all the time."

"Don't you think I know how miserable you were? I was more miserable than anyone," she said, pointing to her heart. "I did everything I could to keep our family together."

"You made a mistake!" I said. I was shouting at her. "Dad was never part of our family. He didn't know any of our jokes or what kinds of food we hated. He's been gone as long as I can remember. Can't you see anything? He brought a shopping bag full of science journals to Yosemite." I gave her a moment to correct me. She started to cry again. I went back downstairs.

I sat down with Charles and Lily to work on the puzzle. It was starting to get somewhere. Weird little figures were appearing—a screaming man, arms outstretched, falling off the tower, a woman with her hair on fire, a dog vomiting. I couldn't seem to keep my hands off it.

Our mother joined us later in her bathrobe and gardening shoes. She was carrying a tray, which she set on the coffee table. On it was a carton of ice cream, a box of candy that had been in our freezer for months, and a few slices of lemon cake that one of our neighbors had brought over. Our mother said, "Dinner's ready!" She smiled. Lily looked up at her, horrified. "It's been a hard couple of day for all of us," Mom said. "So tonight we'll just do whatever we feel like. O.K.? I'm going to fix myself a nice big bowl of rocky-road ice cream for dinner. Yes. Because that's what I feel like having. That's what I think will make me feel good. Now you kids take whatever you like, too. Ice cream, cake, candy. Come on. Let's get started!"

My brother and sister looked at me. I looked at our mother, whose smile was the saddest expression I had seen since my father died. "Chocolate for dinner?" I said. "Why didn't I think of this?" I went to the coffee table. Charles and Lily joined us around the sweets. I took a piece of candy. It was cold and hard. I had to bite it with my molars to get to the inside, which was frozen mocha cream.

My mother took a spoonful of ice cream. "Oh, gosh, that's good," she said. "How's that cake, Lily?"

Lily chewed for a few seconds, then said, "Fine."

Charles reached for a pink bonbon. I said, "You're not going to like that." He put it in his mouth, made a face, and put the remainder back in its brown paper.

For a while, we ate without speaking, as grimly as if we had been eating liver. Our mother forgot about smiling. Between bites, she stared at Mrs. Riemer's gardenias, which were now limp with brown creases in them. Their scent had passed over the edge of sweet into rotten. I was afraid she might cry again. After a few more bites of ice cream, she stood up. "I'm tired," she said, "I think I'll go to bed. Cathy, would you see that Charles and Lily are in their pajamas and in bed by nine? Thanks, punkin. Goodnight, kids."

Lily curled up on the couch and fell asleep, while Charles and I worked on the puzzle. At ten-thirty, we straightened the living room and put the dishes in the dishwasher. Charles went to his room and closed the door. I whispered Lily's name until she was awake enough to walk, then led her up to bed, where she lay down in all her clothes. I folded up the sides of the bedspread to cover her.

I went outside, climbed up on top of the garage, sat down,

and started to cry. I had been crying off and on for the last few days, but this was different. The tears seemed to rush up through my chest into my throat, which became so choked and tight that there wasn't enough room to swallow. I sobbed and gulped, making sounds I hardly recognized as my own. I was not crying because I missed my father. I was not crying about my mother, either, or because I was worried about whether she would know what to do if the car broke down on the freeway or the gutters on the house got clogged with leaves or we ran out of money. I cried about Professor Minnikel's motorcycle helmet. My father had bought someone a present.

I wiped my wet face on my T-shirt and looked at the view. The fires were still burning up in the hills. I could see a couple of orange spots glowing in the distance. Occasionally the patches of flame appeared to dim, but then the spots brightened again, moving and changing shape as they made their way across the slopes. Some people who lived up there had used the water from their pools to soak the roofs of their houses, hoping to protect them from stray sparks that blew from unpredictable directions.

I pictured what my father might have bought for us, if he had been the kind of person who bought presents for his family: a Frisbee for Charles, a tropical fish for Lily; a nice key chain or an alarm clock for our mother. I would have liked a new barrette.

Perfect Combinations

The night Luke met Denise, she slept in his bed. Not that it was love at first sight or anything; there just weren't enough beds. Paul, one of Luke's roommates, and Denise work at the Third Rail, a rock club in the East Village, where Denise had put a sign on the bulletin board saying she was desperate to find a place to stay, even if it was only temporary. Paul offered her Luke's room, since Luke was away for three months. He and Rick, another roommate, were on tour with a band called Blue Baby.

It was four in the morning when Luke and Rick got back from the road. Denise was drinking tea in the kitchen. When she told them the problem—that she'd been staying in Luke's room for the past couple of months, and now she didn't have a bed—Rick said, "Good luck, you two. I hope you have a restful night."

When they got into bed that night, Denise said to Luke, "So what's it like being a roadie?" Luke knew she was asking because she was nervous, trying to make it seem as if they were strangers who just happened to be sitting next to each other on an airplane, instead of strangers in bed together.

"It's exhausting," Luke said, mostly to put her at ease, to

let her know for sure that he just wanted to sleep. "What's it like being a waitress?"

"About the same," she said.

They went to sleep being very careful not to touch.

Now Luke and Denise sleep together every night on purpose, and Luke wants to marry her. That first night, Denise had been pregnant, though she hadn't known it. By the time she found out, they'd been lovers for three weeks. When he asked her (only once) who the guy was, she said, "Just a guy I used to know back home who was in town for a while. Just no one." She said she would pay Luke back the money for the abortion, but he hoped she wouldn't. The abortion was two months ago.

If she ever asked him, he'd tell her he decided he wanted to marry her because of the way she looked right after the abortion. Her blond bangs were sticking to her forehead, and she'd put one sock on inside out. Her lips had been so pale, with little flakes of peeling skin. When she came into the room where all the husbands, mothers, boyfriends, and girlfriends were, she steadied herself on the doorframe. She looked as though she'd just woken up—she had, of course. At the time, he hadn't said anything about marriage. He'd just held her hand and said, "You O.K.?" every once in a while. When a matronly Puerto Rican woman gave the lecture about how the women were supposed to take care of themselves afterward, Luke tried to memorize the instructions—showers only, no baths; no strenuous exercise for the rest of the day; no sex for at least two weeks; and so on. They handed out the instructions on a Xeroxed sheet, which he looked over to be sure he hadn't missed anything, then folded and put in his coat pocket.

Before the abortion, they'd made love a lot. (It was Denise who made the first move after they'd slept tensely side by side three nights in a row.) What turns Luke on most about Denise is her smell. Even when she gets home from the Third Rail, he can smell her through the cigarette and French-fry smell that's stuck to her clothes and hair; after her bath, it's still there, too. Now, when Luke catches a whiff of her, he has to force himself not to think about sex. Since the abortion, Denise doesn't want to make love. Whenever he starts to kiss her, she turns her head away and says something like, "God, Luke, can't you even leave me alone for a minute? I'm losing my identity here." Sometimes when he's just trying to be friendly, affectionate, she pulls back and says, "Cut it out."

The first time she did that was the night the two weeks of no sex were supposed to be over. He'd just assumed they'd both want to make love, but Denise said no, she wanted to wait a little longer. A few more days, she said—just to be sure. After that, he waited for her to bring up the subject. When she didn't, he started trying to figure out ways to seduce her. One time, he bought some bubble bath and suggested they get in it together, but right away she said, "Luke, this isn't going to make me want to make love." He said that wasn't what he had in mind; he just thought it would be nice, that's all. Finally, she said O.K., but she wasn't into it. She acted like it was just a normal bath, washing herself with her pink washcloth, pretending he wasn't even there. After he got out, she turned on the shower for a minute to get the bubbles off.

He thought maybe it was the way he looked. After all, at work she was surrounded by rock stars all night. So he figured that maybe he just didn't look cool enough. One afternoon, he checked himself out in the mirror for a long time. The biggest problem that he could do anything about was his hair: it was too long. Everyone had short hair now. Luke asked Rick where to get a good haircut. But after he'd gotten it, the new haircut didn't look as cool as he'd hoped. No matter what he did to it, he still looked like a big, lunky roadie, not a skinny, pale rock star. And it didn't make any big impression on Denise. She said, "Oh, you got one of those haircuts, too." He couldn't believe he was getting so bent up about a stupid haircut.

The last time Luke tried to kiss Denise in bed, she said, "Come on, *don't*," and turned over on her side to face the closet. She told him it wasn't him, it was her; she just didn't feel attracted to anyone right now. She said it was probably some kind of phase. The thing that Luke thought of next— just for a split second—was pushing her out of bed onto the floor, he was so mad. During the hour or so before he could sleep, he couldn't remember a single reason for liking her in the first place.

By the next morning, though, Luke loved her again. When Denise woke up, her makeup from the night before all smeared, and said first thing, "Do you know how to make pancakes?," she looked so cute that Luke got right out of bed and went to the kitchen to find a cookbook. There's a sucker born every minute, he thought. While he was working on breakfast, he made a new plan. He wasn't going to get mad at her anymore. He was going to respect her feelings about not having sex and just take care of her. Maybe if he was really good to her, she'd start being attracted to him again. No matter how tough it got, even if he felt like slugging her sometimes, he'd just have to be patient and keep reminding himself that he loved her. Eventually, if he could keep this up long enough, she would come around.

Luke wishes he had a car, so he could pick Denise up every night when she gets off work at the club. Sometimes he gets in a cab and goes down there to wait for her. It's fourteen dollars round trip, not including tip, but the money isn't important to Luke. And it doesn't bother him that she says, "I can get home myself, you know—I'm not sick or crazy or anything." He knows she gets annoyed when he does these things, but the important thing is that she's safe, that she feels safe because of him.

Tonight, Luke isn't going downtown to get Denise, because he has planned to surprise her by having dinner ready when she gets home—around two-forty-five, he figures. He's making a real home-cooked meal. Denise is a vegetarian—even the sight of meat in a TV ad makes her cringe. Luke has bought a copy of *Whole Foods/Whole Health*, because he'd like to start cooking for them more. The book explains about protein complementation—how certain combinations of foods from different food families balance each other, creating protein that is more whole, more useful to the body. The casserole for tonight is in the oven: chick-peas and brown rice. Luke is washing the lettuce for a salad. For dessert, he has made a pan of brownies, and there's Häagen-Dazs (coffee, Denise's favorite). That's probably too much sugar, though. He'll save the ice cream. Tomorrow, he may make something with soybeans and bulgur wheat—another perfect combination.

Denise is always starving when she gets home. Sometimes they go to the all-night deli across the street and get apple juice, sandwiches, and ice cream to bring back to the apartment. (If it were completely up to Denise, she'd get ice cream and potato chips, and she'd smoke cigarettes before and during both courses.) They spread the food like a picnic all over his bed and watch TV.

Luke is good at taking care of people—that's how he knows he can make Denise feel O.K. about them again. His brother Henry, though he's two years older, needed a lot of looking after when they were kids. Henry is retarded. Because both their parents worked, Luke spent a lot of time making sure that Henry was all right. Henry's a good guy, and he tries hard, but he needs a lot of help. His parents would set up a routine for him, and just when Luke started to believe Henry had it down, he would do something completely off the wall. He'd do something like wander away from school, instead of taking the bus home. Luke would spend the afternoon searching for him, panicky and wondering if he should call his mom at work and tell her to come home.

When they were little kids, Henry used to really get on Luke's nerves. One time, Henry stepped on a plastic model Thunderbird that Luke had just finished building, crunching it into a billion pieces. Luke had been holding a Diet-Rite Cola bottle at the time, and he remembers swinging it high and bringing it down on Henry's head. The bottle didn't cut him or even break, but it must have hurt like hell. Then Henry gave Luke a slap that was probably meant for his face but ended up on his ear. Luke screamed at him, "You idiot! You're driving me crazy. Can't you just act like a normal person for once in your life?" Their father had seen the whole thing. Luke thought his dad was going to kill him, but he only sent them both to their room. Later, their dad came in and said he was taking just Luke out to dinner. Luke was scared.

They went to a coffeeshop downtown. After they got their food, Luke's dad gave him a big lecture. This is how it started: "I want to tell you how families work." He said that each person in a family has some things that the others don't. So everybody has to be aware of what each other person is capable of doing and fill in the gaps wherever they can. When everyone is doing their best, he said, they balance each other just right. Luke said it made him mad the way his dad expected him to be some kind of superhuman just because his brother was retarded. His dad said, "I think you know that's not what I'm asking for." Luke acted mad at his father for a while (he ordered dessert and then didn't eat it), but that was only because he felt so guilty about hitting Henry with the bottle and calling him an idiot. Actually, he sort of liked the idea of what his dad was saying. He thought about how important it was to be on guard for whoever might screw up next and then be able to step in to restore the balance. And that's the way Luke still thinks of families—as a group of personalities that complement each other, like beans and grains.

Luke and Denise fit together, too, but Luke thinks of them more in terms of electricity: he sees himself as the ground wire, while Denise is the hot. He's the stabilizer. Denise tends to get distracted, and sometimes she seems to be living another life inside her head. Every once in a while, she glazes over, spaces right out. He hopes it's not thinking about the abortion that takes her off like that, but whatever it is he's sure he's just the guy to bring her back.

It's two-forty-five now, and the casserole is almost ready. He puts the salad bowl on the table, and sits down to wait at the place he's set for himself. He hears the elevator running—great timing, he thinks—but it doesn't stop on their floor.

At three, he takes the casserole out of the oven, even though Denise isn't home yet. He sprinkles confectioners' sugar over the pan of brownies. He is trying to remember a time when she came home later than this. He stirs the salad dressing again.

At three-fifteen, he is starting to freak out. I'll call the Third Rail, he thinks. Maybe the show is running late, or they had a waitress meeting afterward. He dials the number of the Rail, lets it ring sixteen times, then hangs up.

When Luke first met Denise, sometimes she used to take

the subway home from work. Unbelievable. But Denise said that if she made under ten dollars in tips she didn't see how she could afford to take a cab all the way to the upper West Side. So Luke had given her a twenty-dollar bill to put in a special place in her wallet. He told her never to take the subway home again, and she promised. What if she'd spent the twenty and hadn't told him? He tries not to think about what could have happened. Even though Luke gave up smoking two years ago, he gets a pack of Denise's Merits from the bedside table. The first one is awful, and makes him dizzy. After that, they get better, except that every once in a while he thinks he might throw up.

What is the rational way to handle this? He goes back to their room to find Denise's address book. There are three people he knows she likes at the Rail: two waitresses, Patrice and Donna, and Will, a guy who works in the kitchen. I'll call Will last, he thinks.

Patrice doesn't answer, but he leaves a message on her answering machine. Next, he calls Donna, who was asleep. She didn't work tonight, and she hasn't seen Denise for two days. Luke thanks her anyway. He calls Will, and a woman answers. Luke says he thinks he has the wrong number. She says that's O.K. and hangs up. It wasn't Denise.

At four, it occurs to Luke that if she went to a bar or another club after work, she'd have to get home soon, because the bars are closing now. She's never done that before, but it's a possibility. He waits a few more minutes before he starts calling the hospitals. Halfway through the list, he hangs up again. What if Denise tries to call while he's on the phone?

At four-twenty-seven, the yogurt-and-curry sauce that he poured over the casserole a couple of hours ago is curdled and dried up. There are just two possibilities: either Denise is in big trouble somewhere (and big trouble includes dead) or she is just fine, having a swell time, and hasn't thought of calling Luke. If she is dead or hurt, Luke will have to call her mother, in California. Luke talked to Charlotte Holland once when Denise was working. Mrs. Holland had made Luke promise he'd call her if Denise ever needed anything or got into any kind of trouble. She also made him promise that he wouldn't tell Denise why she'd called. If something bad has happened to Denise, he will never forgive himself. He should have picked her up tonight. Screw the casserole.

At three minutes past five, Luke is sitting in the kitchen with his elbows on the table, his face resting in his hands.

When the bands don't draw well, some of the waitresses at the Third Rail are allowed to leave early. Tonight, Denise and Kate leave at one. Kate asks if Denise would like to see her new apartment, have some tea. Denise says sure, she doesn't feel like going home yet anyway. On the way to Kate's, they buy a bag of Lidos and a bag of Mint Milanos. Denise plans to eat half of each bag before she goes home.

The apartment is tiny, and it's still pretty empty, but Denise loves it even before Kate shows her that the dumb-waiter really works. (It lets in a steady cold breeze, but Kate's going to put a curtain or something over it.) What Kate has here is total freedom. When Denise left California, she told her mother it was because she wanted to have total freedom. She remembers her mother saying, "The only true freedom comes through commitment and responsibility." That didn't diminish one bit Denise's desire to go someplace far away and start her life from scratch.

Kate and Denise are both actresses. Kate wants to get into soaps. She could; she's pretty enough. Denise wants to steer clear of television acting altogether, because that's what her mother used to do. She plans to audition for stock companies in New England. She's already worked on a couple of monologues.

Denise has spoken to her mother only twice since she got to New York: once to say that she got here and once to say where she was staying. She gave her mother the phone number of her place on the condition that Charlotte would never call her unless it was an emergency. Charlotte has written Denise thirty-three letters (the last two are still unopened on top of one of Luke's speakers), and Denise hasn't written her mother any.

Denise is careful not to talk about her mother, because it's a whole scene that she's glad to have left in California. What Denise doesn't want to talk about is that Charlotte is famous. Or was. In L.A., when people find out who Denise's mother is, they say "You mean 'Cindi'? How could she be old enough to have a daughter your age?" Everyone remembers Charlotte as the teenager she played for five years in a television series. Denise was born the year after Charlotte got out of her contract, and six months after she got out of her marriage to Robert Holland, the show's producer-director. After the divorce, Charlotte moved back to her parents' house near San Luis Obispo, and she's still there. Denise and Charlotte lived on the money from the *Cindi* series (shown in reruns here and in twenty-two foreign countries). Every few years, Charlotte sues her ex-husband for more money.

When Denise thinks about being at home, what comes to mind is her mother's and grandmother's voices asking her eighty times a day, "Where are you going, honey?" "What are you doing?" "Is that all you're wearing?" She told them a million times they were choking her with concern. By the time Denise got to high school, she didn't even have to say that. She'd just grab her throat with both hands, bug her eyes out, let her tongue droop out of her mouth on one side, and make gagging sounds. "O.K., O.K.," her mother would say. "Just do what you want. I'll pretend I don't know you."

Her mother's mission in life, since Denise was born, has been to prevent her from becoming an actress. Charlotte has always made a big point of telling Denise how many different careers there are in the world. Pouring wine at dinner, she would say, "You could be a vintner. California wineries are now considered to be among the best." When Denise made a pair of men's pajamas into pedal pushers and wore them to school, her mother wrote to the Fashion Institute of Technology and Parsons for catalogues. But Charlotte's favorite was dental hygiene. "You could get a job anywhere," she insisted, "and you'd be working with people, helping people."

In her own way, though, Charlotte could be pretty cool. When Denise was flunking eleventh grade because she'd cut too many classes, her mom didn't yell at her or anything. Twice, she stayed up all night to help Denise study for tests. When kids started wearing fifties clothes to school, Charlotte gave Denise all her old Cindi stuff. There was a circle skirt with a telephone pattern on it that was better than anything from the local thrift shops.

After high school and a few months of college, Denise spent some time in Los Angeles. From the very beginning, acting was the only career Denise thought about. She'd always seen herself walking onto a stage, turning into someone else, with hundreds of people gazing up at her, wanting her to take control of their feelings. In L.A., she got one Life Savers commercial, but for some reason it was never shown. Then, to get to where the theatre scene was better, to get away from her mother, and for some other reasons, she went to New York.

One of the other reasons Denise went to New York was that she was trying to forget about Juan. Denise has loved him for two years. She met him at a comedy club in L.A., where she was a waitress and Juan did a standup act every Monday night. They went out together for only seven weeks, and even then it was on and off. Juan always has a lot of girlfriends. It has taken almost all her concentration to reach the point where she doesn't think of Juan every single minute. In the beginning, she just wanted to go back, tell him that she loved him, and wait for him to love her. She used to walk along the streets in tears, she was so depressed. One time she went into a church and pretended to be praying so she could lower her face into her hands and cry. Things got a little better when she found a job and moved to Luke's apartment. At least she had some people to talk to. The only person in New York who knows about Juan is Kate. When Denise was in really bad shape, she and Kate used to talk about him all the time. They still do sometimes, but not as much.

Denise gets up from the floor to throw away the empty cookie bags. They have been watching a Mary Tyler Moore rerun. In the kitchen, above Kate's bathtub, Denise notices a jar of henna. "Hey," she says, holding it up, "want to do our hair?"

"Isn't Luke expecting you?" says Kate.

"It's after three," says Denise. "He's probably asleep by now." Kate shrugs and gets up to put more water in the kettle.

Denise talks less about Juan now, not because she thinks about him less but because she's already told Kate everything she knows about him and everything she feels. Of course, just when Denise had thought she was getting over him, Juan showed up. Right away, she thought maybe he'd come because he couldn't stand being without her. He hadn't; some producer had seen his act and asked him to audition. He stayed only two nights, and Denise spent the second night with him in his hotel. After he left, she felt great for a while—almost high. She kept going over every little thing he'd said and done in the ten and a half hours they were together. Then, when she didn't hear from him, she felt worse than ever. For two days, she called in sick and stayed in bed listening to records on Luke's headphones.

A few weeks later, she met Luke. That was nice, until she found out she was pregnant. It almost seemed as though Juan had some kind of power to keep her from ever feeling O.K. again. She doesn't know how she would have handled getting an abortion if Luke hadn't been around. But since then it has been really irritating the way he's so nice to her when she is such a mess.

In a lot of ways, Luke is like a male version of her mother. If she gets up in the middle of the night to go to the bathroom, he wakes up and says, "Denise? You O.K.? Sure?" She could tell almost as soon as she met him that he'd ask her to stay in the apartment and that what kept him from asking her right away was that he was afraid of scaring her off. When she was pregnant, she knew he was aching to know who the guy was, did she love him—all that stuff. To tell the truth, the sex wasn't that great with Juan. Even so, she's had some very hot dreams about him in the last two months.

Luke has been even nicer to her lately, and that makes it worse. She knows it's mean, but she can't stand the way he's always there, willing to do anything for her, no matter how selfish or extreme the request. Once, very late at night, she said, "I wish I had some really great chocolate," and Luke got out of bed, dressed, and went out. The whole time he was getting ready, Denise was saying, "No, Luke, I didn't mean it. Don't go. I was kidding." Luke was laughing, pulling up his pants, singing, "Whatever Lola wants, Lola gets." He brought back a total of twenty-four ounces of chocolate—six different brands. God knows where he went to get it, how much he must have spent. Does he think that doing this stuff is going to make her attracted to him again? Because it isn't working. Luke tries hard not to pressure her about sex, but then she sees that he's trying not to pressure her, and that feels like pressure. Sometimes when he kisses her hello or goodbye, she almost expects him to say, "See? I'm kissing you in a completely nonsexual way. Let's make love."

Denise's hair hasn't come out very well. Kate's looks pretty good, though. The henna is really for dark hair, not blond, so Denise is now a redhead. She left it on twice as long as the directions said. It's very late, and Denise has to get home. She made just enough money tonight so that she doesn't have to use Luke's twenty.

Uptown, when she sees a thin line of light under the apartment door, Denise feels her stomach tighten. She finds Luke sitting in the kitchen looking exhausted and upset. His eyes are red and his hair is greasy. "What happened?" he says.

"How come you're up so late? It's after five."

"Jesus. Where were you, Denise?" He is getting mad. He's standing up now, staring at her, waiting. "Well?" he yells.

"I'm O.K. I went to Kate's after work—just to hang out. We put henna on our hair. See?"

"Who the hell is Kate?" he roars. "I've never even heard of Kate. I called everyone in your damn phone book. There's no Kate in here." He throws the book over her head into the hall.

"She doesn't have a phone yet," says Denise. "There wasn't anything to write down. What's all this food doing out?" Luke looks at her for a long time, not saying anything. Oh, she thinks, he made dinner for us. She is really sorry, but saying it will probably make him madder.

Luke grabs a roll of Glad Wrap off the top of the refrigerator and starts putting away the dinner. It's all cold anyway, and the stuff doesn't look like it's going to be great reheated.

"I'm sorry, Luke," she says. She can see from the way he looks that it's not enough. "I'm sorry," she says again. He doesn't answer. Something about him is different. Is it because she's never seen him this mad before? Or is it just because he's tired? She picks up the salad bowl to help him, but Luke has the Glad Wrap, and Denise is scared to ask him for it. She puts a plate on top of the bowl and puts it in the refrigerator. "I'm sorry I ruined the dinner," she says.

Luke stops what he is doing at the sink and seems to be staring at the toaster. Denise braces herself for more yelling, but he just says quietly, "Stop saying that, please." Then he gets a garbage bag from under the sink. He opens the refrigerator and takes out the casserole. First, he throws away the Glad Wrap that was covering it; then he turns over the dish. The casserole makes a *plop* sound as it falls into the bag. He puts the dish in the sink. Then he gets the salad bowl from the refrigerator, takes the plate off the top, and puts it in the sink. He lets go of it a little too soon, though, and the plate breaks against the casserole dish. He dumps the salad and puts the bowl in with the other dishes. He scrapes the brownies into the bag and drops the pan with a loud clatter into the sink. He is about to tie the bag when he stops and opens the freezer. He throws in the pint of Häagen-Dazs, too. Denise has to leave the room because she can't stand this. Luke puts the bag outside the front door of the apartment. Then he sits down in the kitchen again and lights another cigarette.

When Denise comes back into the room, she has on Luke's Van Halen T-shirt and her underpants. She is ready for bed. She stands at the door a minute, looking at Luke, until she realizes she's never seen him smoke before. At that moment, maybe for the first time, she really loves him. She goes to him, bends down, bracing herself on his thighs, so that they are face to face. He looks at her. She kisses him. She doesn't want to stop, but Luke pulls away.

He says, "You know something, Denise? Your timing stinks."

Denise goes back into the bedroom. She sits on the edge of the bed and brushes off the bottoms of her feet before she gets under the covers. Then she props up the pillows behind her and takes Luke's copy of *Rolling Stone* from the bedside table. She leans back and opens the magazine. She thinks, So he's a little mad right now.

One Whole Day

Kate and Peter are watching *Entertainment Tonight* on television. Peter is holding their baby, Sam, trying to get him to look at Rod Stewart on the screen. Sam is looking at a pom-pom on the front of his pajamas instead. Rod Stewart announces that Jeff Beck will be playing with him on the upcoming tour. It's true that he and Jeff were not the best of friends when they last played together, Rod says, but they've both grown up a lot since then, and things change.

"Amazing," Peter says to Kate. "Did you hear that? That's practically a miracle. You know what that means? It means anything's possible."

Kate can't remember who Jeff Beck is. The name is familiar, but no face comes to mind. If Peter were in a better mood, she might ask him, "What instrument does he play again?" But Kate and Peter are breaking up, and they are both crabby. Peter is leaving for California tomorrow, and this afternoon Kate accidentally put his denim jacket in with the dirty clothes she took to the laundry. Peter had to go to Mr. Chu's and ask to get the jacket back, so he could take it to California. After that, he barely spoke to Kate until Rod Stewart came on. Since it is their last day together, Kate doesn't want to risk irritating him again by asking about Jeff Beck.

Peter puts his suitcases and shoulder bag next to the front door before they go to bed. Then he reads a book on cabinetmaking, while Kate pretends to sleep. Before long, the baby starts to fuss. Peter picks Sam up right away and walks around the living room with him, a floorboard creaking every few minutes. Peter is saying something. Kate strains to hear him. He is saying, "Hey there, tiger. Hey there, tiger."

The next morning, at eight-ten, Peter says, "I guess I better go," kisses Kate and Sam, and picks up his suitcases. Kate holds the apartment door open for him, then runs ahead down the stairs to get the front door. When she comes back upstairs, she changes the baby and feeds him. Now that Peter is gone, the apartment seems too quiet, as if a background noise—a vacuum cleaner or a fan—had been switched off as he left.

This is the first whole day that Kate has had to take care of Sam by herself. During the two months since the baby was born, even though Kate did most of the work, at least Peter had been around to help. Every morning, he strapped the Snugli to his chest and took Sam out for a walk to the newsstand, where he bought cigarettes and a paper. That was when Kate always took her shower. Now she will have to put the bassinet by the bathroom door, so she can hear him over the water. One of the things she has to figure out is how she will get the groceries up the stairs while she's carrying the baby, not to mention how she will support him if she can't get any acting jobs right away.

The reason Peter has gone to California is that he hasn't had a commission in over a year. He makes wind sculpture. He thinks he might have better luck out West, where there are a lot of gardens and rich people. His last piece was a large sculpture for a department store, which featured it on the cover of a mail-order catalogue. Kate and Peter were sure that this would be his big break.

Right after that, Kate got a McDonald's commercial, followed by one for Kodak. She thought, Now it will be even; now I am successful, too. Then for six months she had a medium-sized role on the daytime soap opera *City of Dreams*. Even when she was pregnant, she got a couple of commercials. When she has her figure back, her agent is going to push for soaps.

Peter's piece didn't lead to anything, and he hasn't made any new sculpture in a long time. Peter has always had trouble deciding what to do about his career. He doesn't know if he should give up trying to be an artist and concentrate on building furniture and making a living, or give everything he's got to his sculpture and resign himself to being broke for a while. For the past year, he has been bartending.

When they first started living together, six years ago, Peter wanted to be with Kate all the time and to tell her everything he was doing, everything he thought. He was in art school then, and sometimes he used things Kate said as ideas for his work. Once, Kate said she wondered at what age people stop making a loud noise when they cry. She and Peter were waiting for a bus, watching a mother try to distract her crying baby. "When do kids stop saying 'Waaa' and start sobbing quietly?" she said. About a week later, Peter made his first wind sculpture. It was two rusted, interlocking iron hoops and a triangular fin mounted on a rod that was connected to a tripod. In the wind, the hoops spun, making a low, metallic, scraping sound. "It's called 'For Crying Out Loud,' " Peter said, after he'd set it up on their roof. "Do you get it? The circles are the mouth, and the sound it makes is the cry. It was your idea, really."

They were married three years ago, while on a trip across

the country. They hadn't planned it, but when they got to Las Vegas and saw all those ridiculous wedding chapels it seemed like the thing to do. They'd had an argument at breakfast about whether to go to Reno or to head straight for San Francisco. Finally, Kate said, "O.K., we'll do what you want, as usual," and got up from the table to pay the check. When she came back to leave the tip, Peter had drawn a cartoon of the two of them on his placemat: Kate with her arms crossed, frowning, and Peter on his knees saying, "Marry me, darling."

Kate put the money on the table and said, "Do you really want to?"

Peter said, "Do you?"

They spent the next fifteen minutes asking each other, back and forth, until the waitress came over and said, "Listen, if you kids don't want anything else, I have other people waiting for this table." Out in the parking lot, they decided to do it.

Sometimes Kate thinks Peter just drew the cartoon to make up with her, that he had no intention of actually getting married.

For almost as long as they'd been married, Peter had been trying to decide whether or not to leave. Sometimes he said that he just wanted to get away by himself for a few weeks to get some work done, that he couldn't concentrate with Kate around all the time. Recently, he had been saying, "If I feel like staying up all night banging on a piece of stainless steel, I don't want to have to worry about waking the baby." Kate suggested that he rent a work space—she would even give him the money. Then he would say, "You don't understand anything I'm saying."

Peter left Kate once before, when he went to a three-month sculpture workshop in North Carolina. He put all his things in storage first, so that he wouldn't have to come back to their apartment. Then the day the workshop ended, he called and said, "What am I doing? I love you. I'm coming home, O.K.?"

Kate said, "O.K." Since then, she has thought, If I had said no, I'd be all recovered by now. I would have been depressed for a while, then I would have been mad at him, then eventually I would have started to feel better.

Last summer, at about the time that Peter said he really was going to leave and Kate finally admitted to herself that they weren't going to make it, she found out she was pregnant. At first, it seemed like the worst possible timing. But Kate had always wanted to have a baby. She thought if she didn't go through with it now, she might not get another chance. When she told Peter, he said he'd stay a few more months, to make sure she was all right. Then he decided to stay through the birth.

Months later, on the bus, on the way home from their third Lamaze class, Peter said, "Maybe we should have a backup coach, in case I want to leave before the kid is born."

Kate stood up and, hanging on to a pole with one hand, the other hand across her big stomach, said loudly to Peter, "You are a useless coward." She got off the bus at the next stop and took a cab home.

The next day, Kate heard Peter tell someone on the phone that he was really looking forward to the birth and to doing his share. Kate knew that he only said it for her to hear and because he felt guilty. But she didn't care what his motives were; she was just relieved that she wouldn't have to have the baby alone.

As it turned out, Peter helped a lot during the delivery— getting her to concentrate on breathing when the pain got so bad she felt she couldn't possibly think of anything else, wiping her face with a cool cloth, even brushing her sweaty hair back into a tight ponytail at one point. When the doctor said the baby was a boy, she caught herself thinking, That's good; Peter will like a boy. Maybe he will stay.

When Sam was a few days old, Peter said he thought he'd stick around, after all. "Who knows?" he said. "I might be a great dad." Sam is now two months old, and Peter is gone. "Look," he said last week, "I admit it's immature, but what can I do?" After that, they didn't talk about it anymore.

Kate plans not to get too sad about Peter's being gone. She's made a list of rules to fend off depression: Don't turn on the TV during the day unless another adult is present; make a date to see at least one friend every day; don't eat junk food except after a respectable meal; don't stay up after eleven-thirty or in bed after eight; and don't play any records older than Prince's "1999" for the next few months. This morning, she is going to clean the apartment so that later she won't come across Peter's magazines and wadded-up clothes and feel sad.

She starts in the bathroom. She takes Peter's dirty ashtray from the windowsill. Ever since Kate was pregnant, he has smoked sitting on the toilet lid, blowing the smoke out the window, because Kate read that inhaling other people's smoke is almost as bad for you as smoking your own cigarettes. She puts the ashtray in the bathtub and turns on the faucet hard to blast it clean. Then she turns off the water, shakes out the ashtray, and puts it back on the sill. Next, she pulls Peter's towels off the bar and dumps them into the hamper. She checks the cabinet for Peter's old combs, medicine, and razors, and throws them all in the wastebasket. Then she cleans the mirror with Windex and the bathtub with Ajax.

She gets one of the stereo-speaker cartons out of the closet and tours the apartment looking for Peter's leftover stuff. She throws in the three art magazines she finds in the living room, a pair of running shoes that she drags out from under the couch, and some books and papers that she finds near the phone and on top of the TV. From the closet, she pulls out a bunch of Peter's coats and jackets, then spreads out her own clothes to take up the space.

Kate goes to the living room to see if the baby is still sleeping. He is. She sits down on the floor next to the bassinet to rest. She wishes the baby would wake up; she would like to have someone to talk to.

Then Kate remembers that she has to change the message on the answering machine. At the moment, it has Peter's voice saying, "Peter Ricco and Katherine Blum are out right now. Please leave your message after the tone." She wants her message to sound cheerful, to say that she's alone and she's doing just fine. She writes down what she wants to say: "Hello. I'm out right now. Please leave your name and number after the tone, and I'll get right back to you." She practices saying this, then changes "Hello" to "Hi" and puts "Thank you" at the end.

Before she speaks, she clears her throat and, for a moment, thinks of herself as Joanne, the character she played on *City of Dreams*. In the scene that Kate is thinking about, Joanne is "radiant," according to the script. Kate reads the message, but when she plays it back it sounds fake. Maybe radiant is a bit strong for an answering-machine tape. She tries the message again but blows the lines and has to start over. Finally, she thinks she's got it right.

The baby is awake, and Kate changes him. It is almost noon—time for *City of Dreams*. Her next-door neighbor, Ernie, will be watching. Sometimes Kate and Ernie watch together. Ernie is a free-lance graphic designer and a workaholic.

He takes one break during the day, to watch the soap opera. The day before yesterday, though, Kate told him Peter was leaving, and Ernie said maybe he'd take the afternoon off today to hang out with her.

Kate puts enough diapers and clothes for the whole afternoon into a bag. She makes herself an egg-salad sandwich to eat at Ernie's. Then for some reason she finds herself hurrying, as if the apartment were about to burst into flames. She wants to get out of here right away. The baby has probably sensed her panic, because he starts to cry a little. She'll feed him when she gets to Ernie's.

When she knocks on his door, Ernie starts singing the *City of Dreams* theme song. He opens the door and says, "Hi, kid," stroking Sam's cheek lightly with his finger. Sam makes a one-syllable sound that is between a cough and a whimper and turns his head away. "Same to you, pal," Ernie says.

Ernie and Kate went to the same high school. They met again a few years ago when, by a fluke, Ernie moved into the apartment next door. Kate couldn't quite remember him from high school until Ernie showed her his yearbook picture. He'd been fat then and looked a lot different. What she remembered about him was Ernie at the senior barbecue, standing on the roof of his mother's yellow Impala belting out the Kinks' song "Lola"—the one about the guy who falls in love with a transvestite. Ernie was holding a bottle of cold duck in one hand and a hot dog in the other. He was making serious dents in his mother's car. He was wearing a shirt made out of Indian-bedspread material; it had belled sleeves. Kate has sometimes wondered if he chose that particular song because he had some idea, even back then, that he was gay. But Ernie says he didn't know for sure until five years ago, when he fell in love with a boy who sold him a half pound of herbed brie in Macy's Cellar. If the senior barbecue had been on a TV show or in a movie, Ernie's choice of song would have meant something. Since it was real life, though, he probably just picked it because it was on the radio a lot then. Ernie is thin now, because he works out all the time.

Kate settles herself in front of the TV. She lifts up her shirt to feed Sam, then takes a bite of her sandwich. Ernie brings a bowl of Rice Chex and a Diet 7UP for himself. He takes hold of Sam's foot in its tiny white sock and rubs it with his thumb. Ernie once told Kate he would like to have a child of his own but won't, not only because he's gay but also because he doesn't want to worry about setting a good example. "Besides," he said, "having a friend with a child is a lot easier and saves wear and tear on the furniture."

Ernie has spells when he doesn't want to see anybody. Sometimes when Kate knocks, he suddenly gets very quiet in his apartment and pretends he's not home. Other times, he opens his door about an inch and says, "Yes?" as if she were a weirdo trying to convert him to some religion, instead of just his next-door neighbor. It's hard for Kate to tell when he's going to slip into his remote mode.

Kate never saw Ernie when she was with Peter, because they don't like each other. Ernie thinks Peter is selfish and childish. Once, Kate made the mistake of asking Ernie for suggestions for Peter's birthday present. Ernie said, "How about a train set? No? A cowboy outfit, then. A pogo stick?"

"Ernie, please," said Kate. "He's my husband."

"Don't snap at me," said Ernie. "You made that mistake all by yourself."

Turning on the TV, Ernie says, "Today, I think Veronica and Jake are finally going to make it into the sack." When she was on the show, Ernie kept trying to make Kate tell him what was going to happen. The main reason he likes to watch is to guess the plot. Today on *City of Dreams*, Dawn's racehorse has been drugged so that he is unfit for the big race. Dawn's mother, Veronica, tries to talk her other daughter, Amber, out of her depression over losing Brian. During a commercial, Kate tells Ernie that in the restaurant scenes the extras don't really talk; they just move their mouths. In the last segment of the show, Veronica and Jake meet secretly at a hotel. Ernie, holding his 7UP bottle, does a little dance next to the TV because his prediction has come true.

When the show is over, Kate puts the baby on a blanket on the floor to change him again. She is afraid that Ernie has forgotten about today, or that he has decided to stay home and work, after all.

"O.K.," says Ernie. "To hell with my career. Want to go on the Staten Island ferry? Then we can go to the movies."

"I thought you'd never ask," she says. Kate is relieved that she doesn't have to go back to the apartment yet. She puts all the baby stuff back into the bag.

The ferry is not crowded, because it is the middle of the day and not very warm. Before the boat starts, Kate opens the bag and puts a sweater and a hat on Sam. It looks like a blue tennis hat and has a row of ducks marching around the crown. Unfortunately, it's too big for Sam and keeps sliding off the back of his head. Sam is oblivious. He has his face all scrunched up, because he is trying to get his fist into his mouth and his sweater sleeve has dropped down over it. The feel of the sweater against his mouth instead of his hand is making him upset. Ernie is laughing at him and tying a knot in the elastic to keep the hat on; Kate frees his hand from the sweater. As the boat pulls away from the dock, Kate says to Ernie, "Would you hold him a minute?" Her shoulders are already aching, just from the trip downtown. Kate passes the Snugli and Sam to him.

"We'll be up front," says Ernie when he's got Sam settled. Ernie sets off while Kate is closing the bag.

When she catches up with them, Ernie is holding the sides of his jacket out to shield the baby from the wind. He is explaining to Sam what a tugboat is. At the moment, Sam couldn't see the tugboat if he tried; he could only see the inside of the Snugli or maybe a little of Ernie's shirt pocket. When they get to Staten Island, Kate and Ernie watch a wave of people hurry off the boat. Another wave takes their place, and in a few minutes the boat lumbers back toward the city. Kate and Ernie walk to the other end of the boat, which is now the front. On the return trip, Ernie tells Sam that the World Trade towers are not the tallest buildings in the world. Kate pretends that the three of them are a family, tourists visiting New York for the first time. As the boat is docking, Ernie suddenly hands Sam to Kate, saying sharply, "Take him. I think I see someone I know."

The movie they pick is *Splash*, which is playing near where they live. Ernie buys popcorn. There are only about twenty people in the theatre. It's air-conditioned, and Kate is worried about the baby's being too cold. She gets his hat and sweater out of the bag again. Ernie says to Sam, "Baby's first movie." Then he says, "Baby's first popcorn," and pretends to offer Sam some.

A few rows ahead of them, a man says loudly to his friend, "I hope that baby isn't going to cry for the next two hours." Kate hadn't thought of that. This is the first time she's taken him to a place where people are supposed to be quiet.

Ernie says loudly, "I hope that man isn't planning to annoy us with his nasal drone during the movie." The lights go down.

Sam is very well behaved for quite a while. He stays awake, but Kate plays with him in the dark, shifting her attention back and forth between him and the movie. Then, during the scene in which Madison and Allen go skating, Sam starts to cry. It's time to feed him again. Kate yanks him out of the Snugli (making him cry harder), hands him to Ernie, pulls the Snugli off, and opens her shirt. As Ernie is returning the baby to her, Sam starts really wailing, and the man in front of them says, "Jesus!" When the baby gets back to Kate, he stops crying. Kate prays that the movie will stay loud enough to cover the sound of his sucking. Her heart is pounding, and she can feel sweat on her upper lip and down the back of her neck. She begins to cry, even though she knows it was really nothing—just some creepy guy in a movie theatre. Ernie takes Kate's hand and kisses it lightly. The kiss leaves a tiny wet drop on her skin that cools in the air-conditioning, then fades away. Kate cries a few more minutes, until she has to blow her nose on a clean diaper from the bag.

After the movie, they stop at the laundry to pick up Kate's and Sam's clothes. Ernie carries the laundry back to the apartment, and Kate carries the baby and the diaper bag. Kate is thinking about what it will be like when Sam is six: He will be learning to read, and he will have friends; Kate will have made rules about bedtime, what TV shows are O.K. to watch, and about eating between meals.

Climbing the stairs is more difficult than usual this afternoon, and Kate thinks maybe she'll try to take a nap when she gets home. She unlocks her door. Ernie follows her inside and puts the laundry on the couch. Just then, there is a noise from the bathroom; it sounds like the window sliding shut. Ernie and Kate stop what they are doing and look at the closed bathroom door. It opens then, and Peter walks out. When he sees them, he jumps with fright, "Oh!" he says, clapping one hand to his chest. "You scared me. I didn't hear you come in."

Ernie says, "I'll see you tomorrow," and leaves.

Peter sits down on the radiator and leans back against the window frame. "I got a job," he says, "and it's right down the street. You know that old shoe-repair place? It's going to be a Tex-Mex restaurant now." Peter explains that he left his bags at his friend Mark's this morning. Then he hung out for several hours at bookstores and coffeeshops; he'd been afraid he'd run into Kate and Sam. He had his interview at two o'clock—he and the owner got along great. "He hired me to build all the tables and the bar. I knew I might get it," he says, "but I didn't want to get your hopes up. If the guy didn't hire me, I was going to stay at Mark's tonight and then fly to California tomorrow. But now we can be together." Peter has the same look on his face that he had five years ago when he told her he knew she would like the red forties dress from the St. Francis Thrift Shop that he'd bought for her birthday. "Surprise," he says, "I'm back."

Kate has an image of herself grabbing him quickly by the ankles, lifting up his legs, tipping him over backward, then letting him fall out the open window. But she doesn't do that.

Peter stands up, stretching his arms toward the baby. Without thinking, Kate steps back suddenly, turning, so that the baby is out of Peter's reach. Peter freezes with his arms out in front of him, a stunned look on his face.

"You'll have to go now," Kate says, and her voice sounds surprisingly loud and firm. "Right away."

Weeks later, there is a postcard from Peter in Kate's mailbox. It's a picture of people wearing bathing suits, rollerskating on a sidewalk along a beach in Venice, California. The message says, "I hope you won't be too disappointed when I tell you this, but Jeff Beck has left the Rod Stewart tour." The card is addressed to Sam.

Trouble People

On the day of the season's first football game, there was a pep rally at Alameda High. The three classes competed to be the loudest-cheering grade in the school. The cheer for Ernie Baird's class was "One! Nine! Seven! Two! The senior class will shine on through!" The cheerleaders on the field were screaming so loud that their faces were red and the veins in their necks stood out. Ernie sat quietly, waiting for the rally to be over and for the lunch period to begin. He was not into sports, and if he had had any school spirit, he would have tried not to act like a jerk about it. Still, for the rest of the day, that stupid cheer rang in his ears as if it were some song he had heard too many times on the radio.

On his way home from school, Ernie stopped at Sanchez's place. Sanchez lived one house down the hill from Ernie and his mother. For five years, since Ernie was twelve, he had been doing chores for Sanchez: getting the mail and feeding the cat while Sanchez was away and gradually taking over the gardening as Sanchez's arthritis got worse. Tomorrow, Sanchez was leaving for New York, so he was going to tell Ernie what to do while he was gone.

Sanchez opened the door before Ernie had a chance to ring the bell. He had on a loose white shirt, khaki pants, and huaraches that squeaked when he walked. Ernie had once bought a pair of huaraches, too, but they hurt, and he didn't have the stamina to break them in.

"First of all," said Sanchez, leading Ernie into the kitchen, "Ted is on a diet." Ted was the cat. "Just give him a half can of Fancy Feast with a small handful of Friskies mixed in and about a teaspoon of warm water to take the chill off. No cat snacks and no milk, no matter how much he begs you." Sanchez reached out to stroke Ted, who lay asleep on a kitchen chair. "You little minx," he said.

Sanchez walked into the living room, beckoning Ernie to follow. Like the house where Ernie lived with his mother, Sanchez's had a living room with big sliding glass doors so that you could see all the way down the mountain, into the valley, over a hill, to the freeway, and out to the ocean. Looking out, Sanchez said, "Sometimes I hate to leave it," and rubbed his hands over his face, as if wiping it clean. He turned again to Ernie and, pointing to the ferns hanging in the window, said, "These, you'll observe, are new. They need a lot of mist." He reached behind the curtain and pulled out a spray bottle, aiming it at a fern and squeezing it twice, to demonstrate.

"O.K.," said Ernie, "lots of mist for these guys."

Sanchez gave him a nod. "The plants in the bedroom should be watered and fed on Wednesday or so. You remember how to do the fertilizer, right?"

"Sure, I know," said Ernie.

"It won't rain anytime soon, so stick to the regular watering schedule for outdoors. Then there's just the mail."

"O.K. Have a good trip," said Ernie, heading for the door.

"Thanks. And listen. You can use the stereo, but I might bring someone back with me, so neatness counts. Bernice will come by to clean a couple of days before I come home, but let's make that an easy day for her, shall we?"

"Right," said Ernie. "I'll make sure I cover my tracks."

Whenever people asked Ernie what he was going to do next year, after he graduated, he said he didn't know yet. But that wasn't quite true. When he'd gone to visit his father in New Mexico last summer, Ernie had asked for a loan to start a business. He wanted to rent a storefront in Santa Cruz to sell T-shirts and fabric silk-screened with his own designs. His dad had said no to the loan, saying that art school or college would be a better idea. Ernie had been mad for a while, but then he'd thought of Sanchez. When Sanchez came back from New York, Ernie planned to ask him for a loan. He had a whole bunch of samples of his work all ready to show Sanchez. Ernie was pretty sure the answer would be yes because Sanchez liked him a lot.

The next day in Government, Ernie was watching Frances Waters. She was probably the reason Mr. Wood was assigning partners for the oral report, rather than letting people choose their own partners, Ernie thought. Frances wore dumpy clothes that made her look middle-aged at seventeen. ("Where does she *get* those sweaters?" "Are those industrial-strength nylons?" Ernie had heard other girls say about Frances.) She had droopy breasts, too, and a little bit of a mustache. She was smart in school. But she hadn't learned that you don't have to shoot your hand up in the air every time you know the answer. And if you know something that isn't in the book, you don't necessarily have to share it with the class. Ernie had his own problems—he was fat—but at least he knew how to behave in a socially acceptable manner, in a way that meant if the class had to pick partners, he would get one.

As if Mr. Wood were punishing him for these thoughts, Ernie got Frances as his partner for the oral report.

Frances slid her desk over next to Ernie's. "I've already thought of a topic," she said. "We can go to the library this week and check the *Readers' Guide* for recent articles." She pulled a notebook marked GOVERNMENT PROJECT out of her bookbag. This is going to be intense, Ernie thought. Do I really deserve this?

The topic Frances had picked was the pollution of the beaches in their town by the oil drilling off the coast. Other people wanted that topic, too, but Frances had managed to clear it with Mr. Wood first. The report was only supposed to be fifteen minutes long, and they had a month to work on it. Frances wanted to get started right away.

Saturday, Ernie watered everything inside and outside and misted Sanchez's houseplants. Then he cleaned Sanchez's garage. "I wish you'd work that way over here," his mother would say, if she knew what he was doing. Ernie had brought his homework so that he could spend the rest of the day here. He put his *Layla* album on the stereo. At home, there was no stereo, so Sanchez let Ernie bring his records over when he was taking care of the place.

Sometimes, Ernie toured the rooms, looking at Sanchez's things, always careful to leave them just as he found them. Sanchez had owned an art gallery in New York before he sold it and moved here to retire. He had paintings by several artists whose names Ernie recognized. Sanchez had even bought a couple of pieces from Ernie's mother, who was a potter. He had paid a lot more than she usually got at the People's Craft Center, where she worked part time and sold most of her pieces.

Ernie sometimes looked in the old desk in Sanchez's bed-room and at the piles of letters in its little compartments. He had taken some of the letters out of their envelopes, his heart pounding hard, as if Sanchez would suddenly appear from South America, Europe, or Oakland and catch him. Some of the letters were written on thin, blue paper in Spanish, which Ernie couldn't understand because he took French. Others contained descriptions of new artists and their work and some-times newspaper clippings.

In Sanchez's closet were some clothes that Ernie wanted to try on: a tuxedo, a cashmere sport coat and a pair of her-ringbone pants that had been made in England, and a stack of ironed pajamas.

Sometimes, Sanchez brought Ernie presents when he re-turned from trips. Ernie's favorite was a box of "trouble people" from Guatemala, six tiny figures in a wooden box. At night, you were supposed to take out one doll to represent each of your troubles, according to the Guatemalan Indian tradition. While you slept, the people were supposed to solve your prob-lems. Ernie tried it once when Ted ran away for three days. It worked: Ted came back the next day, skinny but unharmed.

Ernie did more work for Sanchez than he got paid for. Last year, when Ernie planted the rosemary he found in flats behind the garage, Sanchez called him a prince. He said, "You have added years of life to these old knees." Ernie couldn't wait to hear what Sanchez would say when he saw the clean garage.

As soon as he got home, Frances called to ask if Ernie wanted to get together to make an outline for their report. "I think my mom's going out, so I won't be able to use the car," he said.

"I have a car," said Frances. "Where do you live?"

When Frances arrived, Cynthia went to the door. The first thing Frances said when she walked in was "I love your house, Mrs. Baird."

"Call me Cynthia," said Ernie's mother, smiling. "Let me show you around."

There wasn't much to show, Ernie thought, but his mother always stretched this out. She started with the view out the living-room window, saying it was the reason she rented this place twelve years ago. Recently, the valley had filled up with houses, a development called Rancho Vallejo. Farther away, Cynthia pointed out, were the offshore oil derricks. "Gradually," she said to Frances, "a lot of ugly lights are appearing where there used to be the most peaceful darkness."

"Geez," said Ernie, rolling his eyes, but they both ignored him.

Cynthia showed Frances every room in the house and took her out to the garage, which she used as her studio. Then Cynthia gave her a slice of pumpkin bread, and Frances asked for the recipe. When there was a slight pause in the conversation, Ernie said, "Hey, pardon me, but if we're not going to work on this report, I might as well split."

As soon as Frances had finished a half-hour description of the work she wanted Ernie to do, she walked over to his mother and said, "It was a pleasure meeting you, Cynthia. I hope you'll be here next time I come over."

Ernie waited until he heard her car start before he shouted, "Next time! *Next* time? You try to be a little nice to someone, let her come over and study, and before you know it, she wants to move in."

"Oh, calm down," Cynthia said.

"You made it worse. If I wanted you to adopt her, Cynthia, believe me, I'd just come out and say it."

"I was just trying to be nice."

"To *her*, yes, very nice. But what about your own flesh and blood? And what happened to Ray? I thought you had a date."

"He canceled." Cynthia had been seeing Ray, on and off, for seven years. He was married, so she could never be sure, until the last minute, whether he would keep a date.

On Career Day, Ernie ditched a senior assembly called Career Choices to do some watering over at Sanchez's place. He was out back trimming the wisteria when a car pulled into the driveway. A minute or two later, a guy about Cynthia's age came through the living-room doors into the backyard. Ernie froze for a moment, then said, "Hey."

"How ya doin'?" called the intruder. "I'm George Sanchez, Mr. Sanchez's son." Ernie wouldn't have believed this, except that the man looked exactly like a young Sanchez. "So you're the one who keeps everything looking so nice, huh?" George stretched out his hand for Ernie to shake.

"Ernie Baird. I live up the hill. I work here," said Ernie.

"Well, thanks," said George. "You've done a great job." He paused for a moment, looking around the yard. Then he looked down the hill at some distant point, maybe the antenna of the radio station downtown. He rubbed his face with the same gesture Sanchez had made a few weeks ago. He seemed to be trying to think of something to say. "I'm afraid we've had some bad news," he said finally. "We lost my father a few weeks ago."

"Sanchez?" said Ernie. "He died?"

"Yes. It was very fast, though. He didn't suffer. It was a heart attack. He was on his way to New York. My wife and I were going to meet him at the airport."

Ernie didn't say anything. Sanchez had been dead three weeks. The last time Ernie saw him was almost the last day he was alive.

"Listen," said George, "I'm sure my father appreciated all your work. The place looks great. But for the time being, I'd rather you didn't do anything else, O.K.? Thanks. Say, do you have a key to the house?"

"Sure I do," said Ernie.

"I'd like to have it, if you don't mind."

Ernie reached into his pocket for the key. "But what about Ted?"

"Ted?"

"His cat. Sanchez's cat. I feed him."

George thought a moment. "Would you like to take him home?"

"Sure, but I couldn't," said Ernie. "My mom doesn't like cats."

George said, "I'll figure out something, then."

"There's one more thing," said Ernie. "I have all my records in the house."

"O.K.," said George. "I'll help you get them out."

Ernie got a box from the garage, and they loaded it with albums. Ernie showed him where Ted's food was. "Now," said George, walking Ernie out to the front steps, "how much did my dad owe you?" He reached into his pants pocket.

"Nothing," said Ernie. "He paid me before he left." This wasn't true, but Ernie just wanted to go home now. Halfway down the driveway, he turned around. He wanted to say something else—that Sanchez was the coolest old guy he'd ever known or that the ferns needed to be misted today—but George was already closing the front door.

Cynthia was out in her studio when he got home. It wasn't

until Ernie told her about it that the fact of Sanchez's death started to sink in. "I think he died on the plane," he said. Then, because he could feel his lips quivering and tears beginning to form in his eyes, he started for the house. As he turned, he suddenly pictured a very young Sanchez, standing with George as a small boy in front of a hamburger stand on a hot beach.

Cynthia said, "I'm so sorry, honey." The sound of her sympathetic voice infuriated Ernie for some reason. He wanted to turn around and tell her to shut up and leave him alone. But he kept walking and didn't say anything at all.

Frances had done so much research that their presentation lasted over half an hour. Ernie was embarrassed to sit in front of the class with her. He let everyone know this by acting as if he wasn't very familiar with the material, even turning to Frances once and saying, "What am I supposed to say now?" Everyone laughed, and Frances seemed to enjoy turning the pages of his notes for him and pointing to the right spot. The rest of the report was slightly comical, too, with Ernie acting disorganized and a little clownish and Frances behaving like an efficient schoolmarm. They both got A's. Ernie was relieved when it was over.

At lunch, Ernie was standing with two other guys, waiting for the cafeteria to open. Frances came over and said, "Let's celebrate finishing our report, O.K.? Why don't you come over to my house for dinner?"

One of the other guys said, "Pfff," and turned to face the lunchroom windows, covering his smile with his hand.

"Well, maybe, sometime," Ernie said.

"How about tonight?" said Frances.

"Tonight isn't the best night for me."

"Thursday night, then?"

"I'm going to be really busy with some things for the next few weeks," said Ernie. "Maybe the next month."

"O.K.," Frances said and walked quickly toward the library.

When she was out of earshot, Ernie said, "Try me again in my next life," and the other two guys laughed. A few times during the afternoon, he thought, I hope she didn't get too bummed out.

One night the week after Christmas vacation, Cynthia came home early from a date with her boyfriend. Ray was not Cynthia's type, in Ernie's opinion. Besides the fact that he was married, he was a very straight guy, an advertising executive. Ernie couldn't figure out why she had never married his father, Gary, who was a photographer, an artist like Cynthia.

Ernie was making chocolate-chip cookies when Cynthia slammed the front door and threw her keys into the ceramic bowl on the hall table. Then she turned on the TV, which was strange, because Cynthia hated TV. Ernie came out of the kitchen to see what was going on. Cynthia was sitting there in the dark. She still had her coat on. "Ray is moving to Chicago," she said. "With his wife."

In the light of the television screen, Cynthia's face looked blue and a little ghostly. It was wet because she had been crying. Ernie wanted to dry his mother's face with the dish towel he was holding. Instead, he said sharply, "Ray is a creep, anyway. You're better off."

Cynthia leaned her elbow on the arm of her chair and covered her eyes with her hand.

The phone rang. It was Frances. "Hi," she said.

"Hello," said Ernie.

"How are you?"

"Fine."

Frances paused, then said, "So what's been happening?"

"Nothing."

"Have you applied to any colleges for next year or anything?" she asked.

"No," said Ernie.

"Oh. Well, would you like to go to a movie Friday night?"

"Sorry," said Ernie. "I have a date." This was a lie, but he had to get rid of her.

"I'm not doing very well, am I?" she said.

The following week, Cynthia stayed home and talked on the phone a lot. She told the people at the Craft Center that she had the flu, and as far as Ernie could tell, she didn't go into her studio, either. When he came home from school in the afternoons, the morning paper was still in the driveway and Cynthia was lying on her bed, though he knew there was nothing wrong with her except that she was sad. She put boxes of tissues in the kitchen, in the car, and on her dresser, as if she planned to be sad for a long time.

Exactly one week after Ray told her he was leaving, Ernie came home and found Cynthia practicing typing with a book, *Ten Days to Better Office Skills*, propped up beside her. The newspaper was open to the want ads, and several secretarial jobs were circled.

"Don't you like your job anymore?" Ernie asked her.

Without looking up, Cynthia said, "It's not enough money."

"I thought you said you'd never work in another office." Cynthia didn't say anything. "Didn't you tell me that one time? Cynthia?"

"I changed my mind," she said.

"How come?" said Ernie.

She stopped typing to stare at him hard. "Things are different now." She said this through clenched teeth, moving only her lips. "I'm going to do something else. Will that be all right with you?"

"Excuse me for being concerned," Ernie said, as Cynthia turned back to her typing.

Ernie suddenly realized something: Ray had been giving Cynthia money, and she had hidden this from Ernie. He remembered sometimes seeing Cynthia's checks from her job and from the sales of her work. It only occurred to him now that they didn't add up to enough. The rent on their house had gone up a lot since they moved in. "You're paying for the view," the landlord always said when Cynthia protested the increases. "There are cheaper places." To Ernie, it seemed pathetic to accept money from a creep like Ray just to hang on to a view.

All at once, it seemed to Ernie that there was a kind of slimy lower layer beneath the surface of the people and events that he knew. It had started with Sanchez dying on the airplane, and now Cynthia's taking money from Ray was another part of it. He wondered if everybody else had seen this all along. On the other hand, he thought maybe he alone saw how sleazy even the most normal-looking situation could become.

Cynthia finally got a job working in the office of a group of lawyers. Every night at five-thirty, she would come home and go straight to her room to take off her dress and high heels. She would put on her bathrobe and pad around in her nylons. Most nights, she didn't feel like making dinner, so Ernie would make spaghetti or chili. Sometimes, Cynthia wasn't even hungry and would go to bed before nine.

Frances called again, at the beginning of the second semester. "I noticed you're in Wood's class this time, too, and
I was absent today. Did you get the assignment?"

"Yeah, hold on," said Ernie. "Pages one eighty-six to two
ten. Write a page about how city regulations affect your every-
day life."

"Thanks, said Frances. "You know, you seem kind of down
lately. I was wondering, would you like to talk about it?"

"No," said Ernie. "Bye." He hung up.

Sanchez's house remained empty through the spring. Cynthia had heard at work that George and Sanchez's other son
were fighting over the place in court. Someone had closed
the curtains in the house. Ernie imagined the plants inside,
hanging on wires from the ceiling, all dead, probably a fire
hazard. He wondered about Ted, but he had no way of finding
out whether George had gotten him a good home.

This semester, Ernie's last at Alameda High, he had completely lost interest in school. He would write down all the
assignments, but no matter how he tried to talk himself into
it, when he got home, he couldn't force himself to do his
homework. When he was at school, he hoped no one would
say anything to him. In class, he hoped his teachers wouldn't
call on him. Sometimes, just opening his mouth to talk seemed
like too much trouble. When he tried to think about what
he was going to do after graduation, his mind went blank.

Lately, Ernie was watching a lot of TV, even soap operas.
Since Cynthia was gone all day now, Ernie found himself
ditching his last class to come home in time for a show called
City of Dreams. The characters were always dropping in on
each other, sitting at kitchen tables with mugs of coffee and
talking about their problems. Ernie especially liked it when

the people finally revealed terrible secrets, things they had kept hidden for years. He wished he had a secret and someone he could tell it to and then feel better.

One day, Ernie skipped school entirely. He dropped his mother off at work, then drove all the way down to Santa Barbara, where he ate a burrito under a giant tree next to the freeway. Then he drove a little farther and stopped at Rincon to watch the surfers from the road. He wished he could surf. He wanted to sit out there with those guys, wear a wet suit, float on a board, and know that eventually a good wave would come. On the way home, Ernie heard Elton John on the radio singing "Rocket Man" and had to pull over into the emergency lane to listen to the words. He knew just how that guy felt, shot out into space all by himself.

Close to the end of the school year, Ernie found out he was flunking geometry. His teacher kept him after class one day. "What are your plans for next year?" Mrs. Coehlo asked him.

"I don't have any," said Ernie.

"Why not?"

"I just haven't thought about it very much," he said.

"You know as well as I do that unless you do something drastic, you're going to stay right here at Alameda High." Ernie stared at her with the blankest expression he could produce, hoping she would give up and leave him alone. "Mr. Baird," she continued, "you have only turned in three home-work assignments for this class, and you've failed two out of three tests. If you don't turn in three-quarters of the homework and raise your test grades, I'm going to have to give you an F. I don't think either one of us would enjoy starting the whole course over again in summer school. We have a problem here, Mr. Baird."

"*We* don't have a problem, Mrs. Coehlo. *You* have finished high school and college. You've got a husband and kids and a job. I'm the one who's in trouble."

He could see Mrs. Coehlo fighting an urge to yell at him. "I'm giving you a chance to get yourself out of trouble. You can continue to do nothing. Or you can turn in the homework between now and two weeks from Friday and take the two tests the following Monday after school. If you need extra help before then, I'm in the teachers' lounge most lunchtimes." She picked up a pile of homework and her attendance book and left him staring at a poster of a Möbius strip on the classroom wall.

That night, Ernie woke up from a dream, turned on his light, and looked around for his box of trouble people. He just wanted to see them again. He took out four of them and laid them on the top of their box. They were dressed in pants or dresses made of strings and scraps of bright fabric. Their hair was made of black sand glued to their heads, and their eyes were painted wide open. "Help," Ernie whispered to them. He picked up one doll and said, "Geometry." Then he put it down, picked up the next one, and said, "My mom." To the third, he said, "A job." He held the last one in the palm of his hand for a moment before he whispered, "Frances Waters."

During the last weeks of school, Ernie started getting up early every morning and staying up late to do geometry problems. At lunch, he worked in the library, sitting in a back corner where no one could see that he was eating—two packs of little doughnuts covered with powdered sugar that he pulled, one by one, out of his backpack. At the end of two weeks, Ernie had finished all the homework he needed in order to pass.

On his way to Mrs. Coehlo's room the afternoon he was supposed to take the tests, Ernie walked past the temporary buildings, where all the language classes were. Frances was there, sitting in her car, listening to a Joni Mitchell tape and putting on makeup. She was looking at herself in the rearview mirror and concentrating so hard that she didn't notice Ernie leaning on a dumpster about fifteen feet away. She put on everything: eye shadow and mascara, stuff to make her cheeks pink, and two colors of lipstick, one on top of the other. She studied the effect from several angles, then spit on a tissue and wiped everything off. Ernie walked away then, thinking that it wasn't really fair to watch what other people did when they felt desperate.

He took the two tests back-to-back while Mrs. Coehlo sat at her desk eating a tuna sandwich and copying grades into a spiral notebook. When he had finished, she marked his tests as he watched—a 71 and an 83. "You did it," she said. Ernie didn't smile or say anything, but he felt glad that he had finally gotten himself out of trouble.

Frances was hanging around near Ernie's locker. She was wearing a flowered dress with puffy sleeves and a low, elasticized neckline. She probably made it herself, Ernie thought, "This is my final offer," she said. "Would you like to go to the senior prom with me?" He could tell by the way she said it that she had practiced to make her voice sound casual. It was a hot day, and Frances had big, wet circles under her arms. "I know these things are stupid," she said. "But we could make it fun. Would you go? Just as a goof?"

"Frances, I can't," Ernie said. "I almost flunked a class. They wouldn't let me into the prom. I even got a letter about it from the activities office. I would've had to turn in a note from Mrs. Coehlo by last Friday, and she just gave it to me five minutes ago. But I have to be honest with you. I don't dance, and I hate to get dressed up. So even if I hadn't almost flunked geometry, I would have had to say no."

"Right," she said. "I see what you mean. Don't worry. I won't bother you again," she said walking away.

"I really am sorry," Ernie said. But she didn't turn around.

The senior beach party was held the day before graduation. Ernie wondered if getting to go was worth doing all those geometry problems; there was nothing good to eat. Near the hot dogs, Ernie spotted Frances. He was about to duck out of sight when he saw that several football players were teasing her. "Go easy on that bubbly stuff, Frances. It goes right to your head, you know," one of them said.

"Here, let me freshen your drink," said another, reaching toward her with a bottle of cold duck. Frances was holding her plastic cup at such an angle that wine slowly trickled out onto the sand. It took Ernie a few moments to realize that Frances was drunk.

"O.K., guys," Ernie said, "that's enough."

"Oh, look, Frances, it's your hero, Ernie Baird, coming to your rescue."

"Leave her alone, Fremont," said Ernie.

"Sure, Baird, just watch out your girlfriend here doesn't puke all over you."

The group moved away, but an English teacher came over then. "Listen," she said. "The drinking age in California is still twenty-one. Get her out of here, Ernie, before we all get into trouble."

For a second or two, Ernie considered saying that he and Frances were not together. Then he said, "O.K., Miss Jackson. I'll take her home."

Miss Jackson started to walk away, then she turned around and said, "I hope you haven't been drinking, too."

"No way," said Ernie. "Want to smell my breath?"

"Not especially," said Miss Jackson, and she went over to

relieve Jenny Rosenburg, who was taking instant photos of Senior Sweethearts for $1.50 apiece.

"Come on, Frances," Ernie said. "We have to go."

Frances sank down onto a picnic bench. "I can't go home," she said. "I'm drunk."

"I see that."

"My father will have a cow," she said and started to cry. Big teardrops rolled down her cheeks, and her face was turning red. "I feel terrible."

"O.K., O.K.," said Ernie. "You'll feel better in a little while. And you don't have to go home. We can go someplace else. Here." Ernie handed her a napkin to dry her tears, took the cup from her, and led her to Cynthia's car. His mother didn't need it that night; she had gone out with one of the lawyers from her office.

He took Frances to a party he knew about at Phil Crandall's house, in Rancho Vallejo. Crandall's parents were away on a trip to Europe or someplace. His sister Deirdre had pasted up decorations in the family room—a large cardboard owl wearing glasses and blue silhouettes of a boy and girl in mortarboards. Outside, around the pool, she had strung paper lanterns, alternating with fake rolled-up diplomas. Ernie found lawn chairs for himself and Frances. Crandall was walking around in bare feet, jeans, and a Seafoam Surf Shop T-shirt. He gestured to the decorations. "Isn't this wild!" he said. "Hey, get yourself some food, Ernie, before the surfers get here and scarf it all up. Deirdre made chili."

When he was gone, Frances said, "Could he tell that I'm drunk?"

"No, I don't think so. I'm pretty sure he couldn't." Then, because she looked so sad sitting there, Ernie changed the subject. "So, Frances, what are your plans for the future?"

"College," she said. "I'm going to Cornell. That's back East."

"Oh?" said Ernie. "I have a brilliant career ahead of me also. I got a job at Taco Casa on Mesa Drive."

"You're not going to college?" Frances said.

"Don't look so shocked," said Ernie. "I'll survive. And who can tell? Maybe while I'm spooning beans into tortillas, I'll discover the meaning of the universe." They sat quietly for a few minutes, looking at the pool. The lights were on under the water so that it glowed aqua in the dark. Probably, it was visible from Ernie's house on Sierra Road, where no one was home to see it. "You know," Ernie said, "a friend of mine died this year, and a few other things happened. I guess reality kind of caught me by surprise, sort of sneaked up behind me and bit me on the butt. I used to think I knew exactly what I wanted to do. Now I'm not so sure."

"This year has been hard for me, too," Frances said. "But you probably know that." She looked down at her sandals for a moment. Then she said, "Sometimes I am so lonely."

A few months ago, Ernie thought, it would have been embarrasssing to hear this. Now he knew what she meant. He also felt protected by the fact that she was still a little out of it from the cold duck. "Sure you're lonely," he said. "Everybody is. Why do you think people have parties?"

Frances appeared to be considering possible answers to this question. "So they won't have to feel so lonely?" she said uncertainly.

"You're absolutely right," said Ernie. "It's a very common feeling. But you're not lonely right now, are you? This is O.K., isn't it, here at this party with me?"

"Yes," she said. "This is O.K." A feeble little smile started to form on her lips. "I guess it is."

"I'm glad to hear that," said Ernie. "I feel O.K., too, right at the moment."

Ernie went to the family room to get them some food. Crandall's sister Deidre was putting out bowls. Ernie filled two with chili. "Great party," he said.

"You don't think the decorations are dumb, do you?"

"Dumb?" Ernie said. "Oh no. I think the decorations are excellent." He nodded a few times to convince her.

"Well, thanks," she said. When she went outside to see if anyone needed anything, Ernie went to the kitchen to boil some water. He found a jar of instant coffee and made Frances a cup, black, just like they always did on television, even though he knew from driver's ed that nothing makes a person undrunk except the passing of time.

They stayed at the party a couple of hours, until Frances felt sober enough to go home. Ernie even danced with her once, just to cheer her up. Then later, when he dropped her off at her house, he stayed to watch her walk up the driveway, unlock the front door, and flip one hand backward in a wave before he drove away. He couldn't quite figure it out: It wasn't as if now they were friends, exactly; they were more like two people who'd gone through some scary ordeal together—an earthquake or a shipwreck—and survived. He didn't pass any other cars on the way home, and he didn't even turn on the radio. He wanted to preserve the quiet.

The moon was so bright that Ernie went all the way up Sierra Road without headlights. At the top of the hill, he stopped the car and got out to see if he could find the lights of the Crandalls' pool. There were four pools lit up in Rancho Vallejo that night, but Ernie was sure he had picked out the right one.

Trying to Smile

When my mother was sick, I took care of her. My father talked me out of quitting my job in San Francisco, so for several months I spent a lot of time driving. It was two hundred miles between my place and my parents'. To stretch out my visits, I used vacation time and sick days. At the end, when my mother could no longer bathe or dress herself or even sit up, I took a month off without pay. I was tired all the time and eating too much. But somehow I think I believed that the worse I looked and felt, the more likely my mother's recovery would be. Even with cancer, it is pretty hard to understand that your mother will die, especially if she is only fifty-four and just last year wanted to buy Nautilus equipment for the house. When she did die, it was hard to get used to. Her best friend from college said she would fly to California for the funeral, and I caught myself thinking that I would go to the family room and say, "Guess who's coming!" I pictured my mother sitting there at her desk with a mug of coffee, paying bills.

I didn't cry at the funeral, so afterward everyone said that my mother would have been proud of how strong I was. But that wasn't it. I was too nervous to cry. During the service, I worried that I wouldn't be able to get the food out of the refrigerator and onto the table before the guests started to arrive at the house. I was afraid that I hadn't made enough potato salad and that maybe the plastic glasses that Dad and my younger brother, Phil, had bought were a mistake and would look cheap. Almost the whole day before the funeral, I had been returning the sickroom furniture that we had rented and shopping for a dark dress to wear. I wanted to wear something pretty to the funeral, something my mother would have liked. But I couldn't find anything like that. I ended up wearing a black sweater and a skirt that was too tight in the waist and missing a button. Though I arranged it so that the safety pin was undetectable, these were exactly the kind of clothes that, not long ago, would have really pissed my mother off.

I had imagined that while my brother was home we would spend a lot of time talking about Mom. But we didn't talk about her at all. I spent the whole time doing errands, offering and accepting food, agreeing with everybody about what a good person my mother had been, trying to smile, and then wondering if that was appropriate.

The following weekend, my dad wanted me to help him get rid of my mother's clothes. "We might as well get it over with," he kept saying. But I didn't want to do it at all, ever. I wanted him to ask some of her friends to come over and go through her things so that I could go to my own apartment and be alone. But that would have made it harder for my father, so I tried to act as though it weren't difficult for me. It took us two whole days to sort through everything and decide what to do with it all. Dad took a lot of breaks to go outside, pretending to be making critical adjustments to the sprinkler system so that he wouldn't have to see me stuffing Mom's dresses into garbage bags for Goodwill. I was amazed at how much she had. Since my brother and I had moved out, she had even taken over our closets. My mother had thirteen slips, three of them unworn, and eight bathing suits. Several times, my father said, "Honey, if you want any of this, just take it." I didn't. First of all, most of it would have been too small for me. Second, I had never been the kind of daughter who wore her mother's clothes. It would have seemed unnatural.

For quite a while after she died, I almost missed my mother's being sick more than I missed her being healthy. I had too much time and nothing difficult to do. I joined a health club, tried not to eat, and picked a very complicated sweater pattern to knit. I decided to try for a promotion and started to go to work early and to leave late. But I couldn't get over the feeling that I was still waiting for something to happen. I found a therapist named May and started to talk to her about my life for an hour every week.

One night about a month after my mother died, I was getting ready to go to the Body Shop with my friend Wendy for an aerobics class and the steam room. At practically the same moment that Wendy buzzed me from downstairs, the phone rang. It was my brother. I said, "Can I call you back, Phil? I'm on my way out."

"No way," he said, "this is important. Lizzie and I are getting married on July sixth. Here, talk to Liz."

Then Phil's girlfriend came on. "Hello?" she said. "Isn't it great? We just called my parents and your dad. What do you think? Sisters-in-law. Pretty intense, right? Or is it sister-in-laws?"

"I'm not sure," I said. "The first one probably. Anyway, congratulations. I'm really happy for you."

"Your dad seemed excited about it, too. We're going to have a traditional wedding in Westport, Connecticut, where my parents live. Oh, wait, Phil wants to talk to you again."

"Hi," he said. "Since you're going out, we'll tell you all the particulars later."

"Phil?" I said. "Can I just say one thing?"

"No," he said. "Goodbye."

I know what he thought I was going to say: "Don't you think it's a little soon after Mom died? Why don't you wait?" But I wasn't going to say that. I was going to say, "If Lizzie gets any ideas about my being a bridesmaid, talk her out of it, O.K.?" But Phil had already hung up.

I did count it up on my office calendar the next morning, and the wedding would take place just ninety-one days after our mother's funeral. That night, Lizzie called to ask me to be a bridesmaid. Her mother probably told her it would be a nice idea. Over at my friend Wendy's, I looked it up in *Miss Manners' Guide to Excruciatingly Correct Behavior*. Miss Manners approved of the bride including the groom's sister among her bridesmaids. I had known Lizzie three years, as long as she and Phil had been together, but I didn't feel we knew each other well enough for me to say that I didn't want to be in the wedding. It could hurt Phil's feelings, too. Under the circumstances, I thought, I had better just try to get through it somehow and pretend I was enjoying myself. I wished I had a boyfriend to take with me, though. There is nothing like a wedding to make you feel solitary. I would have even settled for Wendy, if I thought I could talk her into it.

For the next several weeks, I got a lot of mail from Lizzie, asking me to state preferences about various things. There were pictures of dresses photocopied from *Vogue* and *McCall's* pattern books with notes on them saying things like "Does this look too much like a prom dress?" and "Mom loves this, but I think it's a little too severe," and "What about this? Without that horrible ruffle, of course." There were some scraps of material that I was supposed to rank in order of preference, then send back; drawings of shoe styles from which I was supposed to select a favorite; and the question of whether

I would mind wearing something on my head. There were two other bridesmaids: Barb, Lizzie's best friend, and Julie, a cousin. Apparently our tastes differed. I voted for the blue-and-white cotton print dress with an empire waist, pumps, and no headgear. Instead, we were getting the drop-waist pink taffeta with dyed-to-match ballet flats and baby's breath halos. I had to send Lizzie my measurements. Since I was planning to go to the Body Shop regularly, and also thinking about joining the Diet Center (where Wendy had already lost eight pounds), I shaved a little off some of the key numbers. I looked at it as a good form of incentive.

I didn't hear anything from Phil, but he talked to Dad, and Dad talked to me. Dad kept saying, "Your mother was very fond of Lizzie." This was true. The first year Lizzie and Phil were together, he brought her home for Christmas. She and my mother stayed up until two A.M. once, talking. I couldn't believe it—my mother who never went to a New Year's Eve party because she couldn't make it until twelve o'clock. She had cut her finger that day, and she explained staying up late by saying that the cut hurt a lot and kept her awake. But I think she just said that because she knew I was jealous.

A couple of months after that, I was with my mother when she picked out a birthday present for Lizzie. It was a fuchsia angora V-neck sweater, size small, that, even if the store had had one in my size, would have looked completely out of character on me.

My mother used to give me lectures on style. The point was that she had it and I didn't. Part of it was genetics: I inherited my father's stocky build and tendency to gain weight, while my brother got Mom's tall, lean build. But it was more than just physical type. There were rules to be observed. To my mom, using a black purse in summertime was wrong. She also believed that looking good was worth a lot of effort, and I think she even enjoyed working at it. She would go to three or more stores looking for an item like eggshell-colored stockings, or sit in the hairdresser's for two hours having streaks put into her hair and her nails painted to match a dress. I have always found it hard to care about that kind of thing. On the other hand, she could wear blue jeans, a sweater, and a big silk scarf and look dressed up. Though I have gone through stages in which I really tried, eventually I just slump back into wearing the least noticeable clothes available, using the same kind of lipstick and mascara that I bought in high school, and avoiding things like nail polish. My mother was always saying things like "You're not going to wear *that*, are you?" or looking me over and saying, "Maybe a splash of color would help. Try this purple sash." I always refused to take her suggestions, even when I knew she was right. We had a lot of fights about that. Once I said, "Nothing I've ever done counts for anything as long as you think my haircut doesn't complement the shape of my face. Right? Admit it." What my mother called style was one of the things that attracted her to Lizzie, who could also spend whole days shopping, even when she didn't need anything.

When we got home from buying the birthday present, my mother showed me a picture of Lizzie and Phil, ice-skating. Having grown up in California, Phil wasn't any good on ice skates. He seemed to be clinging rather desperately to Lizzie's coat, his shoulders hunched and his hips jutting clownishly to one side. Phil looked panicky, while Lizzie was laughing. My mother said, "Don't you love that little hat she's wearing? Isn't she cute?" She said it, I thought, exactly as if Lizzie were a kitten or a baby.

My therapist said it was perfectly normal to feel resentful about my mother's infatuation with Lizzie. Then she asked what I would like to tell my mother, if she were here right now. I said, "I'm not sure." Then I just sat there for the rest of the session, staring at a wall socket, feeling foolish, and waiting for it to be time to go.

I had to arrive in Westport a couple of days before the wedding. The first thing I thought when I pulled into the driveway was that the Wares' house looked just like something on TV. The house my brother and I had grown up in was a one-story house built during the early sixties on a quarter acre of dirt. My father had moved us there from Wisconsin so that he could open a chain of pizza restaurants. The Wares' house was more in the style of the one on *Father Knows Best*. It had two stories and several big, leafy trees around it.

Mrs. Ware came out to greet me. She was wiping her hands on a dish towel that she had dangling out of one pocket of her culottes. "You must be Deirdre," she said and shook my hand. "Phil is out with Lizzie's brothers doing some errands, but Lizzie's here." She led me upstairs. Lizzie was in the bathroom, pulling rollers out of her hair. "Hi, Liz," I said, and we kissed.

"Hi," she said. She started brushing out the curls and swearing. "I hate my hair."

"Leave your poor hair alone, Liz," said her mother. "Let's have some lunch."

"Lunch? Are you kidding?" said Lizzie.

"She seems to have lost her appetite," Mrs. Ware said to me. She looked at Lizzie's reflection in the mirror and said, "It's just the excitement, sweetie." The two of us backed out of the bathroom and went downstairs to have tuna sandwiches.

Afterward, Lizzie and I had to drive over to the seamstress's house for the fitting of my bridesmaid dress. The seamstress, Bridget, was about my age with very short, spiky hair on top and a long, thin, braided tail hanging halfway down her back. I imagined it wasn't as big a style here in Westport as it was in some other places. Lizzie sat down on a striped cushion on the floor with a copy of *Bride's*, while I went behind a curtain with my dress. It was tight; I had some trouble zipping it up all the way.

When I came out, Bridget said, "You know, it looks like I made this a little small through here." She pinched the fabric in a few places. "No problem, though. I can let it out in time."

I said, "That's O.K. You can just leave it like this." I knew it was my own fault for pigging out too much and not exercising enough, and I didn't think Bridget should have to do extra work because of me.

"Don't be crazy," said Bridget. "You want to breathe at your brother's wedding, don't you?" She had me take the dress off, then she measured me in my underwear, noting the numbers on the back of a card of needles. I was grateful that she didn't say them out loud and that Liz kept her eyes on the magazine.

After we were finished with the seamstress, Lizzie took me to a shoe store in a mall where we bridesmaids were supposed to buy our ballet flats and have them all dyed the same color. Lizzie said, "I picked this style so that you guys could wear the shoes again." I didn't tell her that I don't wear flat shoes and that I couldn't remember the last time I wore pink shoes of any type, because, of course, it didn't really matter.

When we got back to the house, I changed into a bathing suit and a pair of shorts and went down to the beach, which was only about a five-minute walk from the Wares' house. I put on a lot of number-fifteen sunblock, though, because I hadn't been outside much since before graduate school. After a while, Lizzie joined me. All her hair was hidden under a kerchief, and I could see something that looked like plastic wrap sticking out underneath it. "What's on your head?" I said.

"I put some mayonnaise on my hair, and then I stuffed it into a Baggie. It's supposed to make my hair lustrous and satiny."

"What's the Baggie for?"

"To keep the heat in. That makes your hair more absorbent. I hope it doesn't give me pimples." She spread out her towel next to mine, lay on her back, and closed her eyes. "I'm a nervous wreck. I wish this whole stupid ordeal were over."

"I thought you were excited about it." I said.

"I am. I guess I'm excited about marrying Phil. But the actual wedding, well, let's just say it wasn't my idea to do it this way."

"It wasn't? You mean, your parents talked you into having a traditional wedding?"

"No way. My mother keeps saying, 'Why don't you just elope?' It was Phil's idea. I wanted to go to Europe, get married, and take a three-week vacation. That's what we'd always talked about doing. Then after your mom died, he changed his mind and decided we should do a whole formal number. I happen to think this kind of thing is very fifties, and I'm going to feel like a fool on Saturday. I hope it's not an omen about our marriage or anything." She sat up and examined three or four blond hairs on her leg that she had missed while shaving. Then she said, "I hope Phil's O.K. I mean about your mom and all." She lay down again and closed her eyes.

"You want to know what I'm really afraid of?" Lizzie said after a minute. "I'm scared I'll faint in the church. I fainted at my high school graduation and once in New York on the subway. It happens when I'm hot and nervous and have to stand up a lot. Have you ever fainted? It's terrible. You wake up lying on your back on the floor with a big lump on your head and a whole bunch of people staring down at you."

"You know what your problem is?" I said. Lizzie squinted up at me. "You've got stage fright. A wedding is just like being in a play or giving a speech. Once you get out there and start doing it, you won't be nervous anymore. Really. The scariest part is before it happens."

"I guess you're right," she said, doubtfully. "And the wedding will cheer Phil up, even if I do have a horrible time. I'll just keep picturing us a few months down the road, when we're back in our own place again, the thank-you notes are ancient history, the wedding album is shoved in the back of some drawer, and everyone is calling us Liz and Phil again, instead of 'the happy couple.' " She laid one arm across her face. After a minute or so, she said, "I'm too hyper to lie down." She stood up, hung her towel over one arm, and walked back toward the house. "We've missed all the good sun anyway," she said without turning around.

When I came in from the beach about a half hour later, Phil had returned. He was in the living room, sitting in a flowered armchair with his legs dangling over the side, reading a gardening magazine. He stood up when he saw me, gave me a hug, then said, "So how's it going?" and sat down again.

"Lizzie and I went to the seamstress and got my dress fitted. And we bought my shoes."

Phil said, "Great." I considered saying that Lizzie seemed pretty nervous and suggesting that he talk to her. But Phil looked down at the magazine again and seemed to be getting interested, so I went upstairs to take a shower.

When I came down again, I went into the kitchen to see if I could help Mrs. Ware with dinner. Phil was there, cranking the handle of a salad spinner. Mrs. Ware was pulling the stems out of cherry tomatoes and rinsing them one by one under a thin stream of water. Phil lifted the basket out of the salad spinner and showed Mrs. Ware the lettuce inside it. "This O.K.?"

"Fine," she said.

I said, "Can I do anything?"

"I think we've got everything under control here," said Mrs. Ware. "Phil, you don't have to do this. Where's Liz?"

"She's working on her hair," I said.

Lizzie came to the dinner table with wet hair. "You washed your hair *again?*" said her brother Tim.

"By Saturday, you're going to be bald," Scott said.

Mrs. Ware said the minister was doing two other weddings on Saturday. "I wonder if they're always so busy, or if there are more weddings nowadays," said her husband. "For a while there, it looked like marriage was going right out of style. Now I guess it's back in."

"Who are the other two couples?" Lizzie wanted to know.

"I didn't ask," said her mother.

Phil said, "I got a whole bunch of film today. I'm going to take some pictures on Saturday and not just leave it to the photographer we hired." Everyone laughed because this was so typical of Phil. He takes pictures of everything: food, shoes, sand, water, rumpled sheets, doorknobs. Everything, including people, of course. Phil must have hundreds of pictures of our family: pictures of our mother, healthy as well as ill; pictures of our father laughing, thinking, drinking, and weeding; and pictures of me talking on the phone, in a spaced-out daze, eating, sleeping, washing my face, arguing, and walking. Sometimes I think taking pictures is Phil's way of checking out. If he hadn't known for sure that Dad and I wouldn't have allowed it, I think Phil would have taken pictures of the mourners at our mother's funeral, inside the church and later, milling around our living room with plates of food in their hands.

The next night was the rehearsal. The minister told us all in what order we were supposed to enter the church. He told us not to walk too fast and where to stop. Then he told Phil and Liz that when it was time to put the rings on each other's fingers, they shouldn't try to force them over the second knuckle. This can be distracting, he said, and takes too much time. "Don't worry, if you can't get the ring all the way on, it doesn't mean the marriage won't work," the minister said.

Phil and Lizzie said, "O.K.," in unison. They didn't realize that the minister was making a little joke and that they were supposed to laugh.

The rehearsal dinner was at the Wares' house. I wore the blue dress and navy pumps that I usually wear when I have to take a client to lunch. Lizzie's brother Scott had driven to the airport to pick up my father. They arrived just as we were all looking for our names on place cards at the three tables Mrs. Ware had set up in the living room and dining room.

During the dinner, people started tapping on their water glasses with spoons and then getting up to toast Phil and Lizzie. I didn't know anybody really did that. My father kept shooting me looks from his seat across the room next to the Wares and motioning me to stand up and say something. Every time he did this, I shifted my eyes to my salad plate.

Finally, Dad got up himself. His toast started like this: "The first time my wife and I met Lizzie was Christmas three years ago, though I have to say it's hard to remember the time before she joined us." He told the story about the first time Phil brought Lizzie home, when Mom cut her finger, leaving out the goriest parts, since people were trying to eat. What happened was that on Christmas Eve, while Dad, Phil, and

I were out shopping, Mom and Lizzie stayed home. (Phil and I were leaning against jewelry-store counters, I remembered, examining countless pairs of earrings, trying to choose the right ones for Liz.) My mother was cutting up apples over the sink when she accidentally sliced off part of her finger. Lizzie quickly scooped up the little piece of flesh and stuck it back on somehow, then wrapped a dish towel around Mom's hand and took her out to the car. She lowered the passenger seat of the Rabbit and made Mom lie down while she drove to the hospital. Since Lizzie had been visiting us only one day, and Mom wasn't being too clear on driving instructions, she had to stop once to ask somebody's gardener how to get to the nearest emergency room.

By the time Phil and I got home from shopping, Mom was sitting in the living room with a whiskey sour in her good hand, a blanket draped over her knees. This was before she was sick, and I remember being shocked to see her sitting down while Lizzie worked in the kitchen. Lizzie was finishing getting dinner ready, and she had my mother's blood-stained blouse soaking in a sinkful of cold water. I remembered that what really got to me was watching her pick up Mom's wrist and check to see if the blood had stopped soaking through the gauze. I should be doing that, I thought unkindly; I'm the one who is good in emergencies in this family. I said, "Did they give her painkillers, Liz? If they did, a drink is about the worst thing she could have." Everyone jumped all over me, and I had to apologize to Liz, who hooked her finger into Phil's belt loop and stared at me with a stung look on her face. Dad left that last part out of his toast, though.

He wound it up by raising his glass of California chablis and saying, "I'm sure if my wife were here, she would not want us to welcome Lizzie to our family tonight but simply to acknowledge that she's been an important part of it for some time." The room had gone quiet as Dad spoke. He had tears in his eyes, and so did Lizzie and Mrs. Ware. Then Phil stood up, and everyone turned to look at him. He lifted his camera and took a picture of the empty plates on his table. The camera was set at a slow shutter speed, so that it made a long, loud click. Some people laughed, and Phil looked around the room as if he had just been roused from a nap and said, "What? What's so funny?"

Several hours later, I was leaning against a stack of pillows in the middle of one of the double beds in my motel room. The TV was on with the volume turned all the way down, and I was wondering if there was anything left to read in my bag. Someone knocked on my door. I yelled, "Who is it?" and Phil's voice answered.

"It's me, Deirdre. Open up."

When I opened the door, Phil was holding on to the balcony railing, staring down into the parking lot. His suit was all rumpled and stained as if he had just found it in someone's attic, and his shirt was not only untucked, it was unbuttoned, too. His bare feet looked disturbingly wrong with that suit, like Paul McCartney's on the cover of the *Abbey Road* album, which started all those rumors. He looked and smelled sweaty, as if he had just finished a hundred push-ups or climbed a flagpole or done some other inappropriate stunt. I had the feeling he had come to tell me that someone else had died. He held his watch by the strap buckle and said, sadly, "This broke."

"That's too bad," I said. "What happened to the bachelor party? I thought you guys were going to stay up all night telling gross jokes or something."

"That stuff gets old very fast. I can dance on a tabletop only so long." He glanced behind him at the parking lot for a second, then said, "I'm not getting married."

I didn't say anything at first. The trick to handling emergencies, I have found, is to temper your responses. Exclamations like "Oh my God!" and "Quick! Run!" don't tend to start things off in the direction of resolution. You have to be prepared to absorb emotion or pain or danger—depending on the nature of the crisis—without seeming to be too seriously affected by it. You have to channel your own reactions in the right way or perhaps even suppress them completely. That night, for example, when I heard Phil say he didn't want to get married, I was nearly overcome by two conflicting urges: to close the door in his face, get in bed, and go to sleep; and to scream at the top of my lungs. But I didn't do either. I just waited.

"I'm just not going to do it, that's all," Phil said, coming into the room. He pulled a chair over to the side of the bed. The wooden arm popped off in his hand, and he smacked it back together before he sat down. "I mean, I'm still too sad about Mom. I can't get married when I feel this sad. Can I tell you something?" He smoothed the creases in his pants with a few heavy swiping motions. "I had this really stupid conversation with her a month or two before she died. It was the last time we really talked before she got too sick, and I can't stop thinking about it. I guess I never really admitted that she was going to die. I think I was hoping that you and Dad would take care of it—you know, fix it so she could live and go back to being just Mom again. Anyway, she called one time to ask if I had gotten my car insurance straightened out. She thought I had gotten more coverage than I needed or something, and I told her at Christmas that I would get it changed. But when she called, I hadn't done anything about it. I got all guilty and defensive and said, 'Do we have to talk about this again?' After we argued about it a while, she said, 'Do you think you'll marry Lizzie?' I guess she was trying to be nice, and get off my case, but suddenly it pissed me off that she liked Lizzie so much. I said no. I said we were both too young. Then I told her to quit trying to run my life. She didn't tell me to stop acting like a jerk or anything. She just changed the subject again. She said she was going to ask Dad to plant some more melons, but she couldn't remember what kind she'd gotten last year. 'Remember how good they were?' she said. She probably just wanted us to agree on something. I said no, I thought they were too sweet and reminded her that a lot of them rotted before anybody could eat them. I pictured her sitting in the kitchen with a seed catalogue in her lap, but of course she was in bed in the hospital. I was going to call her back and tell her that I lied and that Lizzie and I really were planning to get married, but I never did it." Phil crossed his arms and let out a long, anxious breath.

"We all knew you were going to marry Liz. Mom knew it, too, whether you told her or not."

"But how do I know I'm not just marrying her because Mom liked her so much? I mean, this whole thing is a joke. I had this idea that my wedding would be a kind of antidote to Mom's funeral. I thought of it on the plane on the way back here. It just kind of mushroomed after that. The guest list kept growing, and the arrangements kept getting more and more elaborate. I still love her, you know, but it's just that the whole thing's turned into this spectacle that has nothing to do with me or Liz."

"So you want to cancel it?" I said. "Do you think that's still possible?"

"Deirdre, come on. You're not going to try to force me to marry her, are you? I mean, we're not just talking about me. We're talking about Lizzie's life, too. Would she be happy, if she knew how sad I am? And what's wrong with living to- gether? It's practically the same thing anyway. You have to help me, Dee. I'm no good at this stuff. Could you talk to Dad for me, please, and say something to the Wares. You know, just to pave the way. I need a hand here."

For some reason, I saw myself making potato salad again and then sitting next to a telephone, checking names off a list titled "CALL." I stood up, and probably my face turned bright red, which happens when I get furious at someone. Usually, though, this takes place when no one is near enough to notice, like when someone takes a parking space I have been waiting for or when I spill a lot of wet coffee grounds on the floor just before I'm supposed to leave for work. I said, "Phil, you are being an asshole." He drew his head back, as if I had slugged him. "I didn't particularly feel like spending my last three vacation days in Westport, Connecticut, and a hundred and fifty-five dollars on a dress and shoes that I don't even like. But I did it because you wanted me to. A lot of people have put a lot of time and effort into something you asked for. Now if you want to cancel your wedding, you're on your own. I'm not doing it for you." I was shouting at my brother, and I expected to hear loud knocking on the wall any second.

Phil stood up and started yelling at me. "I can't believe you said that. I know for a fact that if you had a problem I'd do everything I could to help you out. O.K., O.K., look," he said and brushed his hair back with the heel of his hand. "All I want you to do is tell Dad and the Wares. I'll even write down what you should say. It'll take five minutes. All you have to say is that I've decided I don't want to get married tomorrow and that maybe I'll feel different later, but now just isn't a good time. I'll take care of everything else. I swear."

"No."

"Why are you doing this? You're trying to force me into marrying somebody just because the flowers have already been ordered and it might inconvenience a few people. I really thought I could get your support, but obviously I was wrong."

"Obviously," I said. "I had to pick the damn coffin for Mom's funeral, and I'm not going to cancel your wedding for you, too."

"Oh, give me a break," said Phil. "You could have had help, but you didn't want it. You took over the whole deal, so we could all be amazed at what a saint you are. And that meant making everyone else, including me and Dad, look incompetent. Let's face it, you enjoy doing more than your share and controlling everything."

We gave each other identical unwavering stares—lips pursed, nostrils flared, necks craned up to full extension. It was an expression we had picked up from our mother, who used it on store employees who might try to suggest that an unsatisfactory item was not returnable, or a dinner guest who might start to drink too much, or on her own son and daughter when they tried to get away with lying or spitting or not sharing their skateboards with other children. I did not allow myself to look away, even though I was already starting to feel guilty about refusing my brother's request.

Phil shifted his eyes first, to a hangnail on his thumb. I sat down. When he looked back at me, he said, "So what you're saying is that you think I should get married just because it's what everyone else wants. I should submerge my own feelings so that other people can have a good time and not be upset."

"No," I said. "I'm saying that if you're sure you don't want to marry Liz, then you're going to have to handle it yourself. *You* tell Liz, Dad, and the Wares and cancel all the arrangements."

He thought a moment. Then he said, "You know, I read that after a death you're not supposed to make any major life changes for a full year. The grieving process takes longer than just a couple of months, Deirdre."

"Great. You can tell everybody that you have a panel of experts to back you up."

"God." Phil shook his head in disbelief. Then resolutely he said, "O.K. Fine. I can do this myself. You know something? You're acting like a self-righteous matron."

I said, "Well, you're a jerk." My brother sneered at me and started to leave. "Where are you going?" I said.

"I'm going to talk to Liz. Then I'm going to tell the parents." He opened the door. "See you."

"Phil," I called. He turned around. "They'll all be asleep," I said lamely. He went out and closed the door.

I stood up, then sat down again. I hated these family blowouts, but we didn't seem to be able to get together for any reason without something like this happening. The night of the funeral, after everyone had left and we had all had some of the lasagna that a neighbor brought over, Phil and I sat in the family room, playing Monopoly. Dad didn't want to play and sat in his recliner holding a *Sharper Image* catalogue. Monopoly is pretty pointless with only two people, but we were desperate for something to focus on. For about the first half hour, we sort of mindlessly moved our little pieces around the board, bought whatever we landed on, paid or charged rent, or went to jail with equal resignation. Phil was using the Scottie dog, and I had the iron. Then Phil said something silly in a barking kind of voice, pretending it was the little metal dog talking, and we both started to laugh. It was probably because of all the tension and sadness of what we had been through and just plain exhaustion that we went into hysterics. Then I said something even more ridiculous, an elaboration on what Phil said, which got us laughing even harder, until we were both reduced to idiocy, holding our stomachs, tears rolling down our contorted faces, squeaking out the most ludicrous sounds. Dad tried to get us under control by saying first, "All right, you two." This made us worse. He waited a moment and then said, "Enough. Stop that," in a sharp voice. When we didn't, he said, "God damn it. Don't you have any feelings at all?" Then he left the house, slamming the front door behind him. Phil and I became suddenly silent, folded up the board, and put all the pieces away a lot more neatly and slowly than we ever had before. Then we both went to our own rooms. Dad came back about half an hour later and called, "Dee? Philly?" But we didn't answer. I didn't want to hear him apologize or to say that I was sorry myself, and I just didn't think I could face any more tears. In the next room, Phil was talking on the phone to Lizzie in Connecticut. I turned out my light and lay down on my bed, even though it was only nine-thirty and I still had my clothes on. In the morning, we got up early because Phil had to go to the airport. We all pretended to have amnesia, acting as though what had happened the night before was completely forgotten.

After Phil stormed out of my motel room, I couldn't go to sleep. Now the wedding wasn't going to happen, and I felt it was my fault. I shouldn't have blown up like that. Maybe if I had been more cool about it, he would have changed his mind. I expected the phone to ring any moment. It would be Lizzie. It would be Mrs. Ware. Or it would be my father in tears. I sat up in bed a long time, waiting. I even opened the curtains to see if any cars were approaching my part of the motel. Finally, I put on my Walkman and listened to a Rickie Lee Jones tape until my batteries started to go.

When I opened my eyes, it was light, so I got up quickly and drove over to the Wares' house. Phil, Lizzie, Tim, and

Scott were sitting around the breakfast table. They looked as though they had been there a long time. There were a couple of cereal boxes, some cold toast, and a lot of dirty dishes on the table. Phil was squashing several grains of sugar against the table with the back of a spoon. As I walked in, he was saying, "Mick works out for a couple of months before every tour."

"Deirdre," said Tim, "we were just about to call and wake you up."

"What time is it?" I said.

"Almost eleven," said Lizzie. "Did you sleep well?"

I looked at Phil. He seemed to have adopted the amnesiac posture and was pretending to be really concerned with the consistency of the sugar he had just crushed. "Yeah, fine," I said. "So how's everything going?"

"Everything's going according to plan," said Phil a little unnecessarily. I could see for myself that the crisis had passed. Tim got me a cup of coffee. Maybe to drive home his point, Phil said, "Come on, Liz, make room for Deirdre," and pulled Liz out of her chair and onto his lap.

Mrs. Ware came in and said, "I want this kitchen immaculate by the time the caterers get here. I've already cleaned it up twice this morning." When the dog scratched on the screen door, she said, "We're going to have to put that animal somewhere before this afternoon."

We all started cleaning the kitchen, and Phil waited until the dishwasher was running before he broke family tradition by mentioning our fight the night before. "Sorry, I was an idiot," he said. "I'm just going to do it and try not to think about it too much. Being married is just like living together anyway."

I wanted to say something, but Tim yelled from outside, "I could use a hand from the groom here." He was starting to clean the lawnchairs with Formula 409 and paper towels. "Phil, you slug, this is your show."

Phil walked out the screen door, letting it slam behind him. "Very nice," he said, looking down at the chair Tim was working on. "But you missed some bird doo up in the corner there." Tim sprayed Phil's foot with 409.

During the next few hours, everyone went crazy, trying to get ready. Scott was responsible for getting the video equipment. He called in a panic from the store and said that they had screwed up the order; nothing would be available until the next day. Mrs. Ware swore into the phone, then called several other places until she found one that had equipment, gave her credit-card number over the phone, then called Scott back to tell him where to pick up the camera.

Lizzie burst into tears because she couldn't find the three pairs of panty hose she was sure she had bought. I drove to the drugstore in the shopping center to get her some. They were out of the kind she wanted so I had to decide which would freak her out more—if I took an extra half hour to find the right ones, or if I came back right away with a substitute. I decided to speed back as soon as possible. I had also bought her some smelling salts, and I showed her how I would keep them hidden in the sash of my dress, just in case.

She said, "Wow, thanks. I'm so glad you're here."

I put on my dress, which really was more comfortable now, and drove Lizzie to the church, picking up the other bridesmaids on the way. Mrs. Ware didn't want the church parking lot clogged with a lot of cars before any of the guests even got there. Barb and Julie were wearing shorts and carrying their dresses on hangers. Julie had her hair in rollers. Lizzie had washed hers one final time that morning and then decided to just wear it straight. There was a room behind the minister's office assigned to the women for changing. On a table in the center of the room were some paper cups of cold coffee with cigarette butts floating in them. "This place is disgusting," Lizzie hissed, and I started gathering up the garbage and stuffing it into a paper bag.

Later, as we walked down the aisle in our assigned order, Dad leaned out of his pew to get a better look at me, then gave me a big, misty wink. I tried to smile. During the ceremony, Phil was fine and did everything just the way he was supposed to, even giving Lizzie a reassuring squeeze every now and then. Once he turned stiffly to look at me, and I made the smallest nod to let him know that he was doing well. He looked pleased with himself and turned back to Liz.

I started to cry then and couldn't stop. I was looking at the back of my brother's head and the little circle of wild hair that never seemed to be going in the right direction. When he was in kindergarten, my mother used to try to force Phil's cowlick to lie flat by combing it with water. Standing there in the church, I thought of the tantrums Phil used to throw when he didn't want to go to school and the way my mother used to kneel down to his level and calmly talk him into it. When he stopped crying, she would kiss him goodbye, and then kiss me. I looked forward to that moment every morning because I loved the way her lipstick smelled. Then she would say, "Hold his hand at the crosswalks, Deirdre." On the way to school, Phil and I didn't say much. Every once in a while, he would sort of hiccup and shudder from all the crying. A couple of times, he held my hand the whole way, not just crossing the streets. I was a lot taller than he was in those days, and I would look down and see his hair starting to spring up, so that by the time we got to school, it was as if our mother had never touched it. Near the end of the ceremony, I had to hold my breath to keep from sobbing out loud, but since tears were actually dripping onto the flowers of my bouquet and down my neck onto the front of my dress, I probably didn't fool anyone.

After we had all marched out of the church, Mrs. Ware took me into the bathroom in the parish hall and hugged me for a long time, patting my bare back where the dress scooped down and saying, "I know. I know, dear. You miss her. Of course you do." She helped me safety pin my bra straps to the inside of my dress, so they wouldn't show in the pictures. Then she had to call the caterers back at the house and tell them not to let the dog out of the laundry room.

Mr. Ware had hired what he called a combo to play at the reception. He kept coming over to where Scott, Tim, and I were sitting on the grass stuffing ourselves with cheese puffs and cake and saying, "I thought you kids liked to dance." Then Mrs. Ware would come by and say, "Don't worry. The band leaves at five. Then Scott can drag the stereo speakers outside."

At seven most of the guests had left. Mr. Ware and my father were talking about a downward trend in the computer industry. Mrs. Ware was sitting next to her husband with her shoes off and her eyes closed, holding a can of Diet Coke. When I walked by, she looked up and said, "Is it over yet?"

I found Phil and Lizzie upstairs in her room, looking at a salad bowl they had just taken out of its wrapping paper. They had already changed back into their jeans. "Deirdre," said Phil. "I hardly got any pictures of you today." He picked up his camera and aimed it at me, saying, "Don't do that with your face." The camera clicked, and Phil rolled his eyes and said, "Great. Just what I need, a picture of Dee trying to smile."

"Phil," I said, "I think you guys better get your suitcases and leave for the hotel, so everyone can throw rice at you."

"*That's* it," Phil said. "I couldn't figure out how this thing was ever going to end. Are these clothes O.K., do you think?"

"You look fine," I said and went to find some rice.

Mrs. Ware and I washed glasses until ten-thirty. When the last one was clean, she said, "Now we can go back to normal life."

"Do you think they'll be happy?" I said.

"What a question. Of course they will. Anyway, our job was the wedding, and that's over. The marriage is their problem, as far as I'm concerned. I hope Scott put that umbrella in the garage or it will be covered with caterpillars by morning." She peered out the kitchen window, but it was too dark to see anything. Then she said goodnight and went upstairs.

I went back to the motel and got right into bed without even reading anything or turning on the television. I turned out the light quickly and shut my eyes. This was going to be the beginning of a new phase for me; I was trying not to worry.

The First Weekend

The Saturday Scott moved in with me I was kind of tense. On the way to pick him up in Cambridge, I had to drive around the Alewife Rotary three times before I dared to plunge out of the circle and into the oncoming traffic. I was afraid I would get to Scott's and he would say that he had changed his mind, that he didn't want to move in, after all. Or he wouldn't be there, and no one would know where he had gone. Neither of those things happened, though—Scott was sitting on the front steps, waiting for me. He kept waving at me as I parked, as if I were sailing into a harbor and he were standing on the dock, welcoming me into port. When I opened the car door, we kissed, and he said, "You're here."

We only had to make two trips to my house, using my car because Scott's had died on Storrow Drive the week before. He had sold his bed to the woman who took over his room, and his bureau was missing two drawers, so he threw it out. As we were driving, Scott kept saying, "I'm excited. Are you?" I would say, "Yeah, me too." On the second trip, I said, "I've never lived with anybody before. A boyfriend, I mean, and on purpose." We had already talked about this; we were just chattering out of nervousness.

When we got to my place, we put his stuff away, meaning

we stacked his boxes on top of mine. After three months in the apartment, I still hadn't got around to unpacking everything.

For dinner, I made pancakes, which had always been one of my specialties. This time, though, they kept sticking to the pan. When I finally made a good one, I put it on a plate, set out some butter, syrup, a napkin, and a fork, and said, "Scott, dinner."

"Andrea, it's a work of art," he said. "God damn," and sat down and ate it. Every once in a while, he would say, "Mmm, great." He took small bites to make it last longer.

While I was clearing out some space in the bathroom for Scott's stuff, I heard him doing something in the kitchen. I thought, One pancake is sort of a meager dinner. About ten minutes later, he walked into the bathroom with a sandwich on a plate and handed it to me. "Bacon and peanut butter on toast," he said. "Old family recipe. It's the only thing I know how to make."

I sat down on the toilet lid and ate it while Scott watched me. "You like it?" he said. "Really?" When I finished, he took the plate and said, "You know that pumpkin you have on the kitchen windowsill? Well, it's getting kind of soft."

"We'd better throw it out, then," I said.

"Right, chief," said Scott. A few seconds later, I heard the pumpkin thump into the garbage can.

Before I met Scott, I was going to carve that pumpkin for Halloween. I bought it in a hardware store, where I went to get curtain rods for my new apartment. I thought that with a jack-o'-lantern at least I would have a friendly face at home to look at. But I never got around to making it.

The last group house I lived in had split up in August, because of marriage, new jobs—that kind of thing. I found an apartment over a dentist's office in Watertown. One of my housemates, Charlie, offered to help me move in. Then, when the day came, he grumbled about what a hassle it was and made fun of the gold wallpaper in the bathroom. Years ago, Charlie was my boyfriend, then he was my friend, but recently our relationship had reached an all-time low. He rented a house by himself in New Hampshire, saying that just once in his life he would like to be able to open the refrigerator and know for sure that nothing he wanted to eat would have someone else's name on it.

While all this moving around was happening, I realized that I was sick of my job. I had worked for twelve years for the Case & Holland Publishing Company as an editor of college textbooks. At the time, I was working on a geology book targeted for the junior-college market. During the meeting to launch the project, Art Rogers, our marketing manager, announced that the book was to include no words over three syllables.

I pointed out that the word "geology" had four syllables.

Art paused to empty two packets of Sweet 'n Low into his coffee. Then he said, "Andrea, what I want you to do with this book is sex it up." He described ideas for boxes and chapter openers about earthquakes, gold mines, and landslides, but I wasn't listening. I was thinking, How has it happened that my purpose in life is sexing up a geology book? How has it happened that at age thirty-four I live alone in a one-bedroom apartment and don't even have my own couch?

On the way home on the subway and bus, I listened to Bruce Springsteen on my Walkman. I had it turned up to 8. It came to me then that you didn't have to be in prison, a steelworker, or a laid-off lumberyard employee to be desperate enough to want to burn something to the ground or get in your car and drive away until everything you ever knew was gone forever. You could get just as desperate sitting in a cubicle next to the supply room at the Case & Holland Publishing Company as any one of those guys named Eddie or Wayne that Bruce sings about.

The next day, when I saw a notice in our employee newspaper that there was an opening for an editor in the department that published biographies, I took it down the hall to my friend Eileen. "Read this," I said. "I want that job."

Eileen looked at it, took off her glasses, and said, "You want to know what will happen? They'll interview you about thirty times and then hire somebody from Houghton Mifflin."

"But I guess it's worth a try," I said.

"Not really," said Eileen. "Not when you think about how disappointed you'll be when you don't get it. I'm just being honest, Andrea."

That night, Charlie called. When I told him about the biography job, he said, "Now you're talking! So long, chapter summaries and study guides. Hello, human race!" We stayed on the phone for half an hour, going over what I should include in my résumé and highlight in my covering letter. "Remember," he said, "don't settle for anything less than a big office with a river view and your own secretary."

I got the job. My office was a tiny cubbyhole overlooking the parking lot of the steakhouse next door, and all eight of us shared one overworked editorial assistant who didn't know how to type. But now I felt so much better that I decided I would try a few other things that I had never even considered before.

I called Cambridge Learning Center and asked them to send me their course list. My first choices, Cooking with a Wok and Stress Management, both had waiting lists, so I ended up with Poetry Writing for Beginners. There I met Scott. During the second class, he handed me a piece of paper that at first I thought was a poem. It said, "Want to go out for coffee after class? Scott Ware, behind you and to your left." When I turned around, he lifted a hand off the desk, smiled at me, and turned bright red. I had recently promised myself to say yes to every invitation, just in case it might change my life forever, so I nodded and smiled back.

We went to a coffee shop on Mass. Ave. and sat there, talking, until twelve-thirty. When he drove me home, we sat in the car for about an hour, still talking, with the engine running for the radio and the heater. Then I said, "Well, I guess I'd better go. Work tomorrow, you know." He touched my wrist with the tips of his fingers, and we started kissing. It was almost three before I finally went upstairs. From my bedroom window, I watched his little red taillights all the way down Mount Auburn. I was in love.

The next day, Eileen and I were eating falafels in a conference room with the door shut. I told her about Scott. Eileen said, "Go for it, Andrea."

"He's young," I said.

She said, "Chronological age is a meaningless concept. How young?"

"He's only twenty-three."

She said, "Go for it," again.

For the next couple of months, Scott and I saw each other every day. At work one Monday morning, I walked over to the College Text Division with my coffee. "Eileen," I whispered at the entrance to her cubicle, "I'm thinking of asking Scott to move in with me."

"Do it," she said. "You're in love, he's in love. Do it."

"What about his parents?" I said. "They might freak out when they find out how old I am. For that matter, what about my parents?"

"To hell with all four of them. They're already married."

I felt a little bit guilty about falling in love when Eileen was still alone. She was quite a bit overweight, it's true. But she was also pretty and had a great personality and gorgeous red hair. Despite her many attractive qualities, though, Eileen had never had a serious boyfriend as long as I had known her. As I turned to leave, she said, "Just do it, Andrea."

I also talked to Charlie about what I was planning. This conversation didn't go as well. First, I told him I had a boyfriend. I said, "You'll like him. He's really funny and nice."

"What does he do?"

"Well," I said, "at the moment he's working in a photocopy place, but he plans to go to graduate school next fall."

"Oh, yeah?" Charlie said. "How old is he?"

I considered using Eileen's line about how age is meaningless, but I knew Charlie would just give me a hard time. "Twenty-three," I said.

"Christ, Andrea. You're kidding, right? Please tell me this is a joke."

I said, "Scott's moving in next weekend. I wanted you to know about it."

Charlie said, "Maybe you're not ready to hear it now, but this is going to be a big mistake. You're important to me, Andrea. I don't want you to make a fool of yourself."

"Can I tell you something?"

"Go ahead."

"I'm happy."

"Bull. You could have lived with me, you know." He hung up without saying goodbye.

The morning after Scott moved in, Eileen called. "How's it going?" she said.

I was watching Scott pound a nail into the kitchen wall to hang up a framed poster. A long crack in the plaster was making its way to the ceiling. "Great," I said. "Fine."

"Maybe I'll come over in a while and visit."

Scott turned around to mouth the words "Who is it?" I tried to mouth back "Eileen," but he didn't get it. He tipped his head to one side and lowered his eyebrows: "Who?"

"Eileen," I said out loud, and then into the phone, "Please do. Any time."

After Scott took my car to go to Cambridge and look at bookshelves, I lay down on the floor and took ten deep breaths, in through my nose and out through my mouth. I was trying to relax. Living together wasn't as easy as it looked. When the doorbell rang, it made me jump so suddenly that I heard something snap in my neck.

It was Eileen, carrying a plant. "Hi," she said, thrusting the plant in my direction. "Late housewarming."

"Wow," I said. "Nice. Thanks, Eileen. You didn't have to do that."

"I know," she said. She was out of breath from the stairs. "But I wanted to." She took off her coat and scarf. "I saw Scott out front. He said he was going to look at bookshelves. Very homey. So where's all his stuff? Your place looks exactly the same to me." I pointed to the boxes. "That's *it*?" she said, laughing.

I made some coffee, and we sat down in the kitchen. "Where do you think we ought to look for a bureau for Scott?" I said. Eileen prided herself on always knowing where to shop for things.

"I'd definitely go secondhand on that one," she said. "Look in the *Phoenix* and get something from a B.U. or Harvard student. You don't want to invest too much, in case—well, whatever."

I had been counting on Eileen not to assume that Scott and I would break up. When she changed the subject to complain about the author she was working with, I didn't bother to change it back. I made more coffee and put the plant between the two windows in the living room. Before she finished her second cup of coffee, Eileen said, "I have to go." She took her coat down from the hook, put it on, and looped her scarf around her neck. She seemed to be studying something on the floor. I looked, too, expecting to see a bug or a quarter. Then I realized that there was nothing on the floor and that Eileen was crying.

"Eileen?" I said. "Is something wrong?" Stupid question. It was like saying, "Did you hurt yourself?" when somebody stubs a toe on a coffee table and shrieks in pain.

Eileen managed to squeak out, "Yes," making it a three-syllable word. She put her hand over her mouth and sobbed. I took her by the shoulders and steered her into the living room to our one chair.

"What is it?" I said. Eileen and I had spent a lot of time together, but I had never seen her cry.

"I'm never going to meet anybody," she said.

"Oh," I said, "don't be silly. Of course you are. That's the dumbest thing I ever heard." I sounded exactly like my mother. Before I met Scott, I cried a lot, too. When I really hit bottom, I used to call my mother. Sometimes it helped and sometimes it didn't. "Take off your coat," I said to Eileen. "We'll talk about it."

"I'm sorry," she said. "I'm really happy for you. I'm just sad for me." Her face contorted again and a fresh batch of tears rolled out.

"Eileen," I said. "You're going to meet somebody really great. Soon. I know you are."

"Why is it taking so long?" she said.

"I don't know," I said, patting her back. I leaned down to try to see her face, but she buried it deeper into her hands.

"Because I'm fat."

"If you were perfect, you'd just be intimidating." She didn't look up.

We didn't hear Scott on the stairs—he wanted to surprise us. He flung the door open, leaped into the room, came to a very loud landing beside us, and said, "I'm back, and I'm bad." Then he saw Eileen's face, blotchy red and streaked with mascara. "Oh," he said. He looked at me. I tried to make a face that would express the idea "She's a little depressed. She'll be O.K. soon." Scott didn't get it. I wondered if after many years of living together our nonverbal communication would improve. Scott pointed to his chest, pointed to the bedroom, and went there, closing the door behind him.

"I'm thirty-eight," said Eileen. "I haven't been on a date in a year and a half."

"It's not easy to meet people in Boston," I said.

"You did."

"That's a good point. It's possible. I'm thirty-four. I already have a varicose vein. I didn't think I was going to meet anyone, either, but I did."

"That isn't going to happen to me, and you know it," said Eileen.

"It could. Sure it could. Maybe you should take a poetry course," I said, smiling. She didn't smile back. "Maybe some other kind of course, then. Or a club. You could join a club of some kind." Eileen just stared blankly at her hands. "You have to be open to it, Eileen. You can't just keep telling yourself it's never going to happen."

"I've tried that," she said. "I've tried expecting to find someone; I've tried *not* expecting it. Nothing works." She looked up, as if challenging me to contradict her.

The phone rang. Scott came out of the bedroom and went into the kitchen to answer it. I heard him say that I was out at the moment; then he closed the door.

"It feels hopeless, but it isn't," I said. I patted her again, and we listened to Scott's muffled voice in the other room. Then, as he came out of the kitchen, I said to Eileen, "I'll get you some Kleenex."

In the bedroom, Scott said, "What happened?"

"She's afraid she'll never find a boyfriend," I told him, taking the Kleenex box from the bedside table.

"Oh," he said. "That's rough. Poor Eileen."

"Who was on the phone?"

"Charlie," he said. "I invited him to dinner tonight. He said he'd bring dessert."

"Are you crazy?" I said.

"Don't jump down my throat. He sounded lonely. What was I supposed to do?"

"Next time, try taking a message. The only reason he agreed to come over is so he can call me later and dump on you."

"Very positive attitude you have there, dear. Maybe he just wants to be friends."

"Don't call me 'dear' in that sarcastic tone. I hate it." We stared at each other for a couple of seconds. "I have to get back to Eileen."

While Eileen was blowing her nose, I said, "Scott invited Charlie over for dinner."

"You're kidding," said Eileen. "That's nuts. Charlie will sulk the whole time."

"Maybe I could call him back and cancel," I said.

"Don't," said Eileen. "That will only make it worse. Charlie would never let you get away with it anyway. You're stuck." She laughed, then she patted me. "I have to go. Sorry about the melodrama."

When Scott heard us at the front door, he came out. "Hey, Eileen," he said. "We're having Charlie over for dinner.

Maybe you could come back and join us. I'm making my famous spaghetti."

Eileen looked at me. I smiled. "Well, sure, I guess," she said. "O.K. It beats staying home and dusting my miniblinds. See you around seven or so? Great."

Scott and I said goodbye and waved. After I shut the door, I glared at him.

"Oh, come on," he said. "I just want to be friends with your friends. It'll be fun."

Charlie and I hadn't really been in love, except maybe briefly at the beginning. We saw each other a lot the first year I was at Radcliffe, and even after things cooled off between us we never managed to let go of each other completely. When he needed a date or bodyguard for some terrifying family function, I would go with him. In the last couple of years, if he was low on money, sometimes Charlie did free-lance work for me at Case & Holland. Often when I complained to my mother about not having a boyfriend, she would warn, "It might be hard to meet anybody new with old Charlie hanging around." For a while, I was seeing a man named Hank, one of my other free-lancers. One morning when I came home from Hank's, Charlie burst into my room and said, "Andrea, why are you doing this to me?"

For all the time we spent together, it wasn't always clear where we stood. Once, long after Hank, I tried to get into bed with Charlie. I walked into his dark room and sat down next to him, lifting the covers and sliding my hand down his warm, bare back. Charlie said, "Give me a break, huh? You don't want to do this. Go back to bed, Andrea." I felt like a fool, retracting my arm from under his blankets, so I never told him that that night he was the only person I could imagine being with forever.

Our house gave a party before we all went our separate ways. I had to go outside at one point to divide the bottles and cans from the rest of the trash. Charlie followed me to the garbage cans, though at first I didn't realize it. The music was loud, and I was worrying about complaints from the neighbors. Charlie said, "Andrea?" He walked toward me, leaned very close, squeezing my shoulder, and said hoarsely, "You're the best friend I have."

"Hey, take it easy," I said, and pushed him away from me. I thought he was drunk. I watched my hands, fingers spread, sink into the cable-stitch pattern of his sweater. As he walked quickly back up the porch steps, I realized that I had made a mistake. Charlie wasn't drunk; he was probably just feeling lonely and sad because the house was breaking up, and wanted me to tell him that he was my best friend, too.

After the party, he avoided me and started telling everybody that he wanted to live in the country. I found him in the kitchen one night and told him I was sorry. He said, "Forget it," without looking at me, and then asked if he could have a couple of my peppermint tea bags. He had a stomach ache.

Scott had never made spaghetti before. He got the recipe off the back of the spaghetti box. "You don't have to do anything," he said. "Just relax. It was my idea. I'll make dinner." He came back a few minutes later with an onion in one hand and a bread knife in the other and said, "Just tell me one thing. When they say, 'one half cup onion, minced,' how do they mean that, exactly?"

He needed a lot of help. He had forgotten to buy the mushrooms, so while he drove back to the store I made the salad and the garlic butter for the bread, and set the table. Then when he returned, I showed him how to cut the mushrooms. Before I finished doing the first one, he said, "O.K., O.K., I got it," and took the knife out of my hand. When the mushrooms were all sliced—and still rather large, it seemed to me—he dumped them into the tomato sauce without sautéing them first.

"Scott!" I said. "What are you doing?"

"What?"

"You're supposed to cook them in butter or oil first."

"Oh. Well, does it really matter? I mean, can't we do things a little differently sometimes?"

Charlie arrived in his big orange down jacket that he had had for at least eight years. I remembered that when he got it the Velcro on the pockets was still a novel thing. He was carrying a freezer bag from Steve's Ice Cream. He said, "Smells like snow." He meant the weather.

Scott came out of the kitchen wearing a pink apron my grandmother had made for me. On the bib it said, "Kiss the Cook" in embroidered script. He had just put it on as a joke while I was letting Charlie in.

"Cute," Charlie said without the slightest trace of a smile. They shook hands. Then Scott took the apron off and handed it to me.

"Charlie, Scott. Scott, Charlie," I said. Scott put the ice cream in the freezer, and I hung up Charlie's jacket.

"So," said Charlie, shoving his hands deep into his pants pockets, "how did the first weekend turn out?"

Scott called from the kitchen, "It's not over yet."

Charlie eyed the boxes against the living-room wall. "Gee," he said. "I love what you've done with this room."

"Want something to drink?" I said. "We have red wine, club soda, and orange juice."

"Yeah," he said. "I thought you'd never ask. A beer would be great."

"We don't have any beer. Just red wine. Sorry."

"If it's all you have," he said, and shrugged.

In the kitchen, Scott was stirring the sauce. "Not the greatest sense of humor," he said.

"I guess he's just nervous," I said.

Handing Charlie his wine, I said, "Eileen's coming, too." Charlie didn't like Eileen. Once, at a party, Eileen had questioned him endlessly about whether he had decided not to pursue an academic career because his father was a professor at MIT.

"Well," Charlie said, rolling his eyes, "nothing like good times with good friends."

Eileen brought flowers this time. She followed me into the kitchen, where I found an apple-juice jar to put them in. While I was filling the jar with water, she whispered to me, "I'm better." Then she called to Charlie, "How do you like living in the country?"

"It's about the same," said Charlie, "only lonelier."

"Well, I guess that's why you moved there, right?" Eileen said, carrying the jar of flowers to the table in the living room. "Every time I go on vacation, I think about moving to the country. But I guess I'm too set in my ways. I'd probably miss standing up on the subway twice a day, pressed against total strangers." Charlie didn't say anything but sat down in our chair. I brought out some raw carrots, celery, and broccoli with onion dip. "Can I help you guys do something?" Eileen said to me.

"No, thanks," I said. "I think we're O.K."

"Are there any crackers?" Charlie said.

"Sorry, no. We might have some potato chips, though," I said.

"Skip it," said Charlie.

I went back to the kitchen and pretended to be looking

for something in the refrigerator, just to have a reason to be out of the living room.

"Nothing like being scared of your own guests," Scott said. I stood next to him at the stove, and we both stared down into the sauce.

"Ever notice that this apartment lacks a back door?" I said.

"You're only making it worse, Andrea. Why don't you relax and have a good time?"

"I'm trying to. Really." I went back to the living room, where Charlie was pawing through a box of Scott's books. Eileen was sitting on the floor, looking at the pictures in a wall calendar we had just bought.

Charlie held up a social-psychology book for me to see. "Look familiar?" he said. I had edited it several years ago, and Charlie had written the glossary. He opened the front cover and showed me that "Scott Ware" was written with green felt-tip marker on the inside. Charlie smirked.

"Yes," I said. "That book sold well. Want some more wine?" Charlie snorted. He hadn't touched his wine.

Eileen said, "No, thanks. I get too sleepy. It's good, though. This is a neat calendar."

"Scott found it," I said. "Isn't it great?"

Charlie said, "What is it? Pictures of rock stars with all their birthdays?"

I clamped my teeth together and opened my lips the way dogs do when you pull their ears or try to play with them while they are eating. I said, "Charlie, this is my house. Try to behave like a human being, or go somewhere else." Then I spun around and went back into the kitchen, where Scott had the water running full blast for no reason. That made me even madder. I turned it off, twisting the handles harder than necessary.

Scott was standing in front of the stove, where the flame

under the sauce was much too high, so that it was spattering little orange dots all over the place. He was looking into a pot of bubbling water. "Hey, Andrea?" he said. "Should I put the spaghetti in here now? It's boiling."

I said, "Next time you invite people to dinner, why don't you first make sure that you know how to cook the meal?"

"That's not fair," he said. "I'm just barely keeping it together here. And anyhow I'm doing this for *your* friends." We heard Charlie in the hall, getting his coat. The front door opened and shut. "Is he leaving?" said Scott. He had the contents of the package of spaghetti in his hand. "What's going on here? Answer me, Andrea. How much of this stuff am I supposed to cook?"

"All of it," I snapped. I opened the front door. Charlie was already at the bottom of the stairs. "Charlie?" I called. He kept walking. I ran down the stairs and followed him outside. I heard him zip his jacket. "Charlie, come back. I'm sorry." He looked at me briefly over his shoulder, but at the same time he was getting his car keys out of his pocket. I stood there until he drove away, then went back inside.

When the spaghetti was ready, Eileen got the chair and Scott and I each had two book boxes to sit on. Scott and Eileen were relieved to have Charlie gone. Eileen took off her shoes, and Scott put the pink apron back on. I felt guilty about getting so mad. Scott pranced in with the steaming spaghetti on a platter, and Eileen and I caught our breath, afraid that he would drop it. "This is it," he said. "The big event." He served the two of us without spilling anything on the tablecloth. I thought the mushrooms looked too big and pale, but I managed not to say anything.

Eileen said, "This is really good, Scott."

"I made it," I said, only half joking.

Scott put his hand over my mouth and said, "Thank you, Eileen. I'm glad you like it."

The door opened. It was Charlie, carrying a paper bag. Scott pulled his hand away from my face, as if he had being doing something he didn't want Charlie to know about. We all stared at Charlie. "What the hell," he said. "Can't a guy go out for beer? Andrea, you forgot to lock the door." He took a beer out of the bag.

"Nothing like a tall, frosty one, I always say," said Scott. "I'll get you a plate."

"It's snowing," said Charlie, and smiled at Eileen and me.

"Great," said Eileen. "Pray for two feet of it and no work tomorrow."

"No, don't," said Charlie. "I don't have a snowblower yet."

"O.K., we won't, then," said Eileen, and took a sip of her wine.

Scott brought a plate for Charlie and a glass for his beer. "Nice," said Charlie, "but what am I supposed to open it with, pal—my teeth?"

I was afraid the whole thing was going to start all over again, but Scott pointed to the bottle Charlie was holding and said, "Twist-off."

"Oh," said Charlie. "Right." He opened the beer and poured it into his glass. Scott sat down, rubbed my back a couple of times, and smiled at me. I didn't want to hurt his feelings by leaning away from his hand or alienate Charlie by returning the affection. I reached for Scott's thigh under the table, hoping Charlie wouldn't notice. Charlie looked out the window. "Yeah," he said. "It's coming down now."

Scott sighed and said, "I love it when it snows." Charlie turned his head slowly to face Scott, giving him a cold, deadpan look. Scott turned bright red, even around the edges of his ears. He said, "Well, I do. I can't help it."

Charlie took a bite of spaghetti. "This is good," he said to me.

"Thanks," said Scott.

"What kind of mushrooms are these?" said Charlie, again to me. "Are these the ones you get in the North End and have to add water to?"

"These?" said Scott. "No. Star Market."

"Scott made the spaghetti," I said.

"Oh," said Charlie. He ate two large helpings, and we were all careful about what we said.

Scott and I cleared the table. Then Charlie and I dished out the ice cream. Charlie said, "We could all run a marathon tomorrow on the carbohydrates we're consuming." I pictured the four of us in shorts and T-shirts with numbers on our chests, running along, encouraging each other not to give up.

After the ice cream, Eileen and I washed the dishes. Over the sound of the running water, we could hear Scott and Charlie talking to each other. I said, "What do you think they're talking about?"

"You, probably," Eileen said. Then when she saw the look of fear on my face, she bounced her hip against mine and said, "I was kidding. Don't freak out now, when the worst part is over." I faked a smile and resisted an urge to run in and stop whatever conversation they were having. We looked out the window at the snow, which was beginning to pile up.

Charlie came in and said he had to go before the roads got too treacherous. Eileen said she had to go, too.

"Thanks, you guys," said Eileen as they put on their coats. "You'll have to give me your recipe, Scott."

"Yeah, thanks," said Charlie.

We watched the two of them go down the steps to the

front door. Charlie opened it and stood back as Eileen waved to us and went out. I closed the door and ran to the window.

"What?" said Scott. "Are they kissing?"

"Don't be silly," I said.

Charlie was getting a snow scraper out of his trunk. He walked back to Eileen's car and wiped the snow from her windshield while she sat inside with the engine running. He waved to her as she drove away, then cleared the snow off his own windows.

When I was taking my earrings out and Scott was sitting on the bed setting the alarm, the phone rang.

"All right, your little plan worked," said Charlie.

"What plan?" I said.

"You know. To get me and Eileen together. O.K., I'll admit that she's a lot nicer than I used to give her credit for. I asked her out. But I'm doing this for *you*, all right? I am not promising *anything*, understand?"

"Got it."

"Maybe we'll have a good time. Maybe it will be a big drag."

"Whatever happens happens," I said.

"Right."

We hung up, and Scott said, "Who was that?"

"Well," I said, pausing to put my hands on my hips and prolong the suspense, "*Charlie* asked Eileen out. On a *date*."

Scott put his hands over his eyes and said, "Oh, my God. Poor Eileen."

Then the phone rang again. It was Eileen. She said, "Are you ready for the shock of your life?"

I said, "I don't know."

"Your friend Charlie has a giant crush on me. No kidding. He said I had magnetic eyes."

"I'm not shocked," I said. "I'm not even surprised. You're an attractive woman."

"But would you mind if it got, you know, serious?"

"No, not at all," I said. "Go for it, Eileen."

"O.K.," she said. "I think I will. We'll talk tomorrow at lunch." We told each other goodnight again.

I turned out the light and got into bed. I curled up behind Scott with my cheek against his shoulder blade and my arm around his chest. But I was wide awake. I turned over onto my back and lay there stiffly until I was sure that Scott was asleep. Then I got up, went to the hall closet, and rummaged around until I found a long, red, hand-knitted scarf. Charlie had made it for me in college after I showed him how to knit. On my way back to bed, I hung the scarf over the front doorknob so I could wear it the next day.

As P. T.

The first thing that happened after I got to England was that a taxi driver overcharged me by about four hundred percent. It hadn't occurred to me that this might be something to watch out for. I had graduated from college recently, but there were still a lot of things that I had never done. This was the first taxi ride of my life and my first foreign country. So, though it struck me as odd that the driver should keep the meter running while he bought gas, I didn't say anything. And when he stopped in front of my hotel, I gave him a tip on top of the inflated fare, based on the formula suggested in my guidebook.

The day after I arrived, I had an appointment for an interview at The Theatre School, where I planned to study acting. I had called several schools from my parents' home in Massachusetts, and found out that this was one of the few that still had openings for the term starting in a couple of weeks. On the Underground map inside my guidebook, I located the station nearest the school. It was a dot close to the top of the page at the end of one of the long colored tendrils representing the subway system. In the train, I checked each stop against the map to make sure we didn't take any unexpected turns.

The school was in a converted house in a sagging neighborhood. Typed on a yellowed card by the doorbell were the words THE THEATRE SCHOOL, followed in pencil by PLEASE KNOCK. A middle-aged man with long, greasy hair opened the door. This was the school director, Julian James. I followed him into his office, where he pulled a form from a drawer and filled in the blanks with information I supplied. "Christian name?" he said.

What sprang to mind, for some reason, was what we used to call my sister Harriet sometimes, "Princess Priss." I said, "Priscilla," and while he printed these nine letters, I tried to think of the word for the color of his sweater. In a summer drama workshop, I had learned that colors often worked as last names.

"Surname?" he said.

"Teal," I said and spelled it for him, "T-E-A-L." Then he read off a predictable bunch of questions: birthdate, address in America, address in England, schools attended. The interview that followed lasted half an hour. The questions were not surprising or original: Who were my major influences? What plays had I done? What were the acting roles I would most like to perform? How did I go about creating a character? How did I plan to pay the tuition?

Then I did a monologue, a few speeches from *The Glass Menagerie*, including the one about Blue Roses, that I had memorized the day before on the plane. When I was finished, Julian James said, "Right, then. You're in. See you Monday week, shall we?" It wasn't one of those fiercely competitive schools where they take only a small quota of Americans. We shook hands, I thanked him, and suddenly it seemed the wrong time to say that Priscilla Teal was just a character I had made up on the spot to demonstrate my ability to improvise.

There were notices on the school bulletin board about

flats and furnished rooms to rent. I copied some of these down and went to look for a place to live. First on my list was a room on the third floor of a house owned by a Mr. and Mrs. Hoddings-Leigh. It was Mrs. who showed me the room. She leaned against the door, eyeing me suspiciously, her arms folded over her gray cardigan. An old brown rug covered part of the orange linoleum; the wallpaper, with big water-stained regions like continents on a map, had a pattern of orange flowers on a brown background; and the only source of warmth was a small electric heater that Mrs. Hoddings-Leigh said I could use between 7 and 9 P.M. I didn't know how to say that I didn't want to live there. I had never looked for a place to rent before, either. I looked again at the little sink in one corner of the room and wondered if water ever really came out of it. I said, "It's very nice," and gave her two weeks' rent in advance.

By that afternoon, I had put my clothes in the drawers in my new room and was wishing that school would start right away. I longed to have a friend so that I could tell someone what had happened to me at home before I left. My sister Harriet and my boyfriend Matthew had decided to get married. To each other. I shouldn't have been surprised by this, but I was. During the last year and a half or so, Matthew and I hadn't been as close as we once were. Even when we knew my family would be out for a whole evening, he never wanted to pull out the Hide-a-Bed in the family room anymore. I considered this just a phase. And I didn't think much about it when he said we should start seeing other people. Then I convinced myself that he and Harriet were just having a harmless, passing flirtation.

For years, Matthew and I had been preparing for our acting careers. In high school, we had cut every class we could to meet behind the lunchroom and work on the plays we were writing for ourselves and to practice scenes from the classics. With Matt's tape recorder, we had worked on our foreign accents until they were good enough to convince the waitresses at Pizza Hut and Friendly's that we didn't understand the menus.

After high school, we went to a community college in our hometown and every year auditioned for the spring play. Despite all our practice, we didn't always land the roles we wanted. Sometimes we were even reduced to working on the prop committee. But Matthew used to give us pep talks, saying it was good experience. Sitting backstage at the prop table one night, Matthew whispered to me, "Those jokers will all fall by the wayside sooner or later. We just have to hold on until they do. Whatever it takes to make it in the theatre, we're going to do it." And I believed him.

So I was shocked to find out that all that practicing, planning, and waiting had been wasted, in Matthew's case, because now he had accepted full-time work installing kitchen cabinets for his father's business and was settling down near home with my sister. He said, "What can I tell you? I fell in love. But don't let me hold you back." He gave me his half of the money we had saved up in three years of performing comedy routines for local organizations like the New England Bookworms and the Woburn Gourmet Club for Divorced Men. He said, "I want you to use this for acting school. The best ones are in London, and it won't be cheap. I owe you."

"London?" I said. "Alone?"

I told my parents about Matthew's plan, counting on them to talk me out of it, to insist that I stay home, near them. But my mother kept pointing at the front door and saying, "Go!" My father bought me a set of matching suitcases with wheels on them.

When I said goodbye to Matthew and Harriet, I used a

line from my first speaking role in a junior-high comedy about a family wedding, in which I played A NEIGHBOR. I said, "I wish you every happiness." Matthew put his arm around Harriet's shoulders, and they both smiled, relieved.

My first night at the Hoddings-Leighs' I went to bed at nine, right after I turned off my heater. As soon as I put my head down, I started to cry, being very careful not to make any noise. I had bought a box of Kleenex at a drugstore called Boots. Each time I used one, I put it into the little plastic bag I had brought the box home in. This way, I could hide all my used Kleenex in the morning, and Mrs. Hoddings-Leigh wouldn't know how much I had cried in just one night.

The next day, when I discovered you could make overseas phone calls from the post office, I called my oldest sister, Eileen, at her office in Boston. I said, "I have to come home. I hate it here."

Eileen said, "Now, I'm going to tell you something, and you're going to have to trust me on this. A year in London is going to be a lot more fun than living with your parents in Natick, Mass., and watching your sister marry your boyfriend." She made me promise that I would stay for at least the first two weeks of school, as my deposit was nonrefundable anyway. I told her I would try.

When school started, it took me a while to get used to being called Priscilla. For the first few weeks, all the actors were sizing each other up. The ingenues and leading-man types were checking out their competition. I had never played an ingenue. The kinds of roles I usually got were small, comic walk-ons. I played a lot of character roles, particularly cranky spinster types, middle-aged mothers, and lots of old ladies— tiny, unglamorous parts that required peculiar accents, odd mannerisms, unflattering haircuts, and a lot of work. One of the reasons I had chosen The Theatre School was that its brochure promised fairness: "Each student will receive a sizable, challenging role during the course of the year," it said.

The first day, John, another American who had just arrived, asked me to show him how the tube worked and to go with him to buy the things we needed for school. I could not believe my luck. He was tall and pale, with dark moon eyes and a lot of messy, curly blond hair—my type exactly, I thought, and not at all like Matthew. On an Underground platform, he put money in a vending machine and got a red box of candy called Toffets. He said, "I bought these for my best friend in Great Britain." He undid the buckle of my purse, dropped the box in and closed it again. He smiled at me, and I let out an embarrassing little giggle.

After I had shown John the way home, I stopped by the post office to call Eileen again. I said, "Hello, love. How divine to hear your voice," in a sort of breezy version of Mrs. Hoddings-Leigh, if such a thing were possible.

Eileen said, "Don't tell me. You met a boy you like, and you're staying."

"How dreadfully clairvoyant of you," I said. Eileen said she knew this would happen. I planned to work on the accent while I was here because, though it satisfied Eileen, I didn't think it was up to my usual standard.

The first plays were cast, and my group was doing *The Seagull*. I was playing an old housemaid. I tried not to be disappointed. I practiced my shuffle and stoop everywhere: at school, on the street, and up and down the Hoddings-Leighs' stairs. An Australian woman, Karen Graham, was playing Nina. For practice, I memorized her lines and imagined myself stepping into the role at a moment's notice.

Karen stood out, even among the school's many ingenue types. Though she was loud and almost without discipline, she had an undeniable magnetism. Some of the other women tried to copy the way she dressed, buying black bowlers like hers or putting on sunglasses when it rained. But no one else could pull it off. They failed to realize that it wasn't what she wore that made you want to change everything about yourself, it was Karen.

For our first rehearsal without scripts, she refused to wear her rehearsal skirt, instead of her jeans. "I'm an actress," she barked at Julian James. "I can bloody well imagine I've got a skirt on."

Karen didn't know her lines, either. After she made a number of mistakes, Julian scanned the room and said, "Where is Priscilla Teal?" Because I didn't appear in many scenes, I got the job of prompter. I sat down on the floor in front of the actors with a script in my hand. The first time she blanked in a long speech, instead of saying "Line?" the way most actors did, Karen said, "P.T.?"

" 'I am alone,' " I said flatly.

"I am alone," said Karen with feeling. Then she stopped again. "P.T.?"

" 'Once in a hundred years . . .' " I said.

"Once in a hundred years, I open my lips to speak and in this . . . this um, void . . . my sad . . . um, P.T.?"

" 'My sad echo is unheard. And you . . .' "

"And you, pale fires, you do not hear me. P.T.?"

At this point Karen laughed, and before I could give her the line, Julian James stood up. "Enough! Get out. P.T., see that she learns those lines and don't come back, either of you, until they are learnt."

Karen didn't seem very upset as the rest of the cast reassembled for another scene, and we picked up our things and went out. I had never been told to leave a rehearsal before, so for me this was kind of exciting. We went to Karen's place, a former dining room in another large house, where Karen made some tea and Vegemite sandwiches. Because I was leery of Vegemite—Australian yeast paste that Karen had brought from home—she ate both of them.

"This sort of thing happens to me all the time, by the way," she told me. "Directors simply do not like me. Maybe it's something about my face." She examined her reflection in a darkening window. "Bloody directors are all just too ugly to act, and it frustrates them. I mean, look at our Julian. His teeth are rotten; his body is positively pear-shaped. They take out the sad disappointments of their unimpressive lives on their actors, is the way I see it." She put down her sandwich and lit a cigarette, then flicked it hard against an ashtray, though there wasn't any ash yet. "Right," she said. "We'd better begin, hadn't we?" She opened her script and handed it to me. Whenever she lost the thread, which was often, she would say, "P.T.?" the way she had in the rehearsal studio, and I would cue her. Once I forgot to look down at the book to give her the line. "You know all the words yourself, you little twit," Karen said, laughing. "Hoping I'll have an accident, are you?"

"Oh, no," I said, reddening. "I just want to learn as much as I can while I'm here."

Karen said, "Oh, dear," and we went on.

Ultimately, she lost interest in going over the lines. "I can't think of one man at The Theatre School who's even worth flirting with, can you, P.T.?" she said when she was sick of the play.

"John Arendt?" I said. Since that first day, I had been watching everything he did. "I like John Arendt."

She leaned toward me, rubbing her hands together the way flies do with their legs. "*Really?*" she said, grinning and narrowing her eyes. Then she sat back again and said, "Isn't he one of the Americans? From Texas or one of those places?"

"South Carolina," I said. "The tall blond guy."

"Ooo," she said. "Yes, I have some scenes with him in this pathetic insult to Chekhov, haven't I? And what have you done about your seething passion?"

"Nothing," I said, pulling at a hangnail. I was working up to it slowly. I pictured John and me as an inseparable pair by Christmas.

"Well, you must. You absolutely must. Otherwise it's going to be a bloody dreary year."

While I walked home to the Hoddings-Leighs', I practiced saying, "You absolutely must," the way Karen had, leaning heavily on the "l's" and flattening the "u's." From then on, everyone at The Theatre School called me P.T. until it sounded entirely natural, even to me.

The Saturday before performances of *The Seagull* started, Karen and I took the tube to Portobello Road to wander around and buy things. We ran into John as we were coming out of the Underground. While I was trying to think of something to say to him to detain him a moment, Karen invited him to come with us. He said, "Sure. Thanks," and followed her to where people were just starting to mill along the rows of shops and barrows piled with antiques and used junk. Karen saw some utensils being sold out of a cart by a large, sweaty man with a veiny, red nose. She picked up a fork, knife, and spoon and said, "How much for four each of these?"

"Two pounds," he said.

"I see," said Karen, putting them down on the table again. "I can only pay a pound." She smiled sweetly at him and started to look at some dish towels on a coat hanger at the next stall.

"What about one pound fifty?" said the man, but she didn't

answer. "One pound twenty-five," he said and waited. Then he sighed and said, "Right. A pound, then."

Karen looked up and said, "Beaut." As we walked away, she put the cutlery into her bag and said to John and me, "It's not the money, really. I'm just naturally ruthless."

I saw a teapot I liked with a picture of the Queen on it, but I didn't pick it up because I had never bargained for anything before. Karen squeezed herself between me and the woman who was selling it and weaseled the price way down to fifty p. by calling attention to the fact that the top had been broken and glued back together. Handing it to me, she said, "There you are, my dear. No worries." John bought some teacups with no saucers. He took his wallet out to pay, even before asking the price. Karen laughed and called him a simple twit. "A couple of extra pence isn't going to kill me," he said.

The street was becoming more crowded now, making it difficult for us all to walk together. I followed a few paces behind Karen and John. Once I saw John put his hand on Karen's back, gently guiding her past a trio of jugglers and the crowd they had attracted. Just as I was starting to feel jealous, he looked over his shoulder to see that I was still following, winked at me, and put his hand in his pocket. At the end of the street, Karen bought a lamp shade, then insisted that we go all the way back to the beginning so she could get a certain dish towel she had seen.

We also bought a bag of greasy cookies and pastries and took them to John's room nearby. I washed out my new teapot and John's cups while he boiled some water; Karen sat cross-legged on the rug and arranged the pastries on a chipped plate. After I had poured the tea, Karen took a cookie, placed it on her knee, and lit a cigarette. She said, "Want to know why I'm here? True confessions. I'm in exile, actually. I got sacked from the only theatre company in Australia worth fuck-all.

My husband, Kevin, chucked me out as well." I tried not to seem surprised at the fact that she was married. Karen looked at us in mock innocence, blinking. "I was untrue," she said. "Repeatedly." John and Karen looked at each other; I looked at the floor.

There was a long pause before John said, "I just broke up with somebody, too. Lucy. We were living together in New York, and I just sort of packed and left to come here while she was on the road with her rock-and-roll band. Lucy's not real thrilled. She's called me over here a couple of times. But she's seeing a therapist so I guess that should help."

Karen leaned back against the wall and exhaled some smoke. John looked out the window and twisted a button on his shirt. I said, "Priscilla Teal is not my real name." I wasn't sure whether it was my delivery or what, but the two of them burst out laughing. Karen tipped over on her side with her knees drawn up to her chest and laughed silently with her mouth wide open, hardly pausing long enough to draw a breath. John slapped his knee, squinted his eyes into slits, and said, "Haw, haw, haw," very slowly and very loud.

They thought I was joking. I chose to go with it, deciding not to tell them my story after all, and poured more tea for them. Later on, when there was a pause in the conversation, Karen said, "Priscilla Teal is not my real name!" attempting an American accent, and John spat tea all over his pants.

A little while later, Karen and I left John washing the dishes. On the street, Karen said, "He's a bit of a shit, isn't he?"

"John is?" I said.

"Well, leaving his girlfriend like that."

"I guess you're right," I said. "That was pretty mean." But privately, I thought maybe there was a good reason.

"You're still in love with him, aren't you, you silly thing?" she said, punching my shoulder.

"Yes," I said, looking away so she couldn't see my face turning red.

"Oh, he's all right, I suppose," Karen said. "I'm just off men at the moment." This impressed me; I knew such indifference was beyond my scope.

In my room, I forced myself to compose a congratulatory message for a wedding card that I had bought for Harriet and Matthew, who were going to be married in a week. After an hour's work, this is what I had come up with: "Congratulations. I wish you every happiness. Your sister/sister-in-law." I hoped they wouldn't notice that I was repeating myself.

When we were small, Harriet and I used to play a game we called "Here Comes the Bride" that involved our older sister Eileen's white nylon half-slip. One of us would put the elastic waistband around her head, letting the rest of the slip hang down her back. The other would walk slowly and ceremoniously beside her down the aisle between our twin beds, humming "The Wedding March." When we got to the dresser at the end, we would say in unison, "Oh, darling," lean toward each other, and just when our faces were about to meet, scream and fall backward onto the two beds. We did this over and over until our stomachs ached from laughing, and we could barely make it to the dresser before we collapsed, helpless with hysterics.

Most of the time, Harriet wore the slip. She always came up with a reason. "My hair is longer," she would say, "so I'll be the bride." Or "I'm wearing white shorts and brides have to wear white." We both knew from the outset that Harriet would wear the slip more than I would, not because of her hair or the color of her shorts or even because she was a year and a half older than me. It was because I was as obedient and pliable as Harriet was forceful and controlling. The night I wrote the message on the card, I dreamed that I went to Harriet's wedding in the slip. At first this filled me with a deep sense of satisfaction, until Harriet's appearance in a real wedding gown made me feel foolish, sitting there in church with my family, wearing a half-slip on my head.

During the performances of *The Seagull*, Karen was still having trouble with her lines. Between scenes, I would stand in my maid costume in the wings with her and whisper what she had to say the next time she went on. Once she made me go outside with her to do this so she could have a cigarette. That night I didn't hear my cue, and the other actors had to improvise for several long moments while I hurried up the stairs, past the prop table, around a rack of costumes, and onto the stage. During our notes session afterward in the dressing room, Julian James used me as an example to show everyone that missing a cue was "very unprofessional." After he had left the room, Karen said, "Oh, dear, P.T., I hope I haven't spoilt your brilliant career in the theatre."

When our first plays were over, Julian James assigned new groups. Karen and I were in the same one again. Our group's play was *The Time of Your Life*. This had always been a favorite of mine. Even better, I was the only woman in our group who hadn't had a big part last time. Though the plays hadn't been cast yet, I knew I was destined to play Kitty Duval. Evenings in my room, I started developing my character and learning all my lines.

Karen caught a cold and stayed home from school. She missed a special lecture on makeup. The whole school gathered to watch a friend of Julian's, Clive somebody who worked in television, demonstrate tricks for altering people's looks. As he introduced himself, he held a black case that looked something like a doctor's bag. "Now then," he said, his eyes darting around the room. "Upon whom might I experiment?" Many people looked down at their notebooks to avoid making eye contact. "You there," he said, looking in my direction. I glanced left and right. "Hallo," he said. "Yes, you, love." He clapped his hands twice. "Come, come." I went to the front of the room and turned my face upward to let him change me into someone else. He took a long time smearing on foundation, drawing in lines and shadows, even applying some sort of plastic to my chin. I hoped he was transforming me into a sexpot, like the kind of prostitute you saw in musical comedies—with alluringly arched eyebrows, bright red lips, and a lock of hair falling languidly over one heavy-lidded eye. There was the bored buzz of talk in the room as he worked, and I didn't notice anyone taking notes or sketching Clive's techniques. At the end, he handed me a mirror. He had made me into an old hag, complete with a hairy mole on my chin. I could have done this myself. I had certainly had enough practice. John walked into the room then, late as usual. He said. "P.T., you're looking well."

During the laughter that followed, I grabbed Clive's wrist. "Make me beautiful," I whispered hoarsely.

"Sorry?" Clive said, trying to pull away out of my tight grip.

"I want to be *pretty*. Do it." I squeezed harder.

"O.K.," he whispered back through clenched teeth. "All right, ducks, I'll give it a whirl. Just leave go the arm, shall we?" Then, in full voice, he said, "Now we'll do something quite different." I took my hand away, and he set to work, first wiping away the wrinkles, then applying a new foundation. He brushed, smeared, and dabbed various colors on my cheeks, eyes, lips, and even the sides of my nose.

As he stepped back to present me to the school, there were a couple of gasps. Above the murmur of surprised exclamations, I heard John say, "Holy shit."

I looked in the mirror and found myself attractive, just the way I had been picturing Kitty Duval. My bangs were swept off my face, giving it an unfamiliar oval shape. The blue eyeliner Clive used made my eyes look bright green, instead of their usual dull hazel, and my lips were full and shiny, like a model's in a fashion magazine. "Quite the face of a chameleon," said Clive. "Not literally, lucky girl. But she takes makeup well—when an artist knows how to use her, of course."

Julian squinted at me from the back of the room and said, "Lovely," a number of times in rapid succession.

"Right, then," Clive said, packing up his tubes, bottles, and brushes. "That's my miracle for the week. Ta, everyone." I left the makeup on, and throughout the day, people told me how striking I looked, how *different*. Everyone, including Julian James and John, had seen that I could look amazing.

The third day Karen was sick I went over to her place with some groceries. "P.T.," she said when she came to the door, "what a mate." Her voice croaked, and her hair was a blond, tangled mess. She looked ill, but in a pretty way, like someone playing a sick character in a movie.

"We're doing *The Time of Your Life* next," I said. "I love that play. And I figured out that I'm going to play Kitty."

"Oh, really?" she said, pawing through the food I'd brought. "You think so, do you?" I made her something to eat and told her what had been going on at school, leaving out what had happened in the makeup session with Clive because I was afraid she would make sarcastic comments about it.

She was in bed for a couple of weeks, and I got into a

routine of going to see her after classes. She always said, "Was there any post?" as I came in. Usually there wasn't, so I brought gossip magazines or chocolate to try to cheer her up. I had a feeling she was waiting for some particular letter that never came.

Once when I came from the mailbox empty-handed, Karen said, "Christ, P.T., I'm miserable," and turned her face to the wall.

I said, "It's a bad flu. A lot of other people at school have it now, too. Give it a couple more days. A week at most."

"Oh, don't be such a little fool," she snapped. "I'm not miserable because I'm sick. I'm sick because I'm miserable." Then she started coughing like crazy, and I had to get her a drink of water.

One night before bed, I put away my *Time of Your Life* script, put on my coat, and went out for a walk to see if I could say all the lines without looking. Passing the Pig and Thistle, a pub near The Theatre School, I saw the oddest sight: Karen was having a drink with Julian James. She was looking up at him, laughing, and he was smiling down. This struck me as strange, not only because I had thought she was home in bed, but also because Karen couldn't stand Julian.

The next morning the cast lists for the new plays were on the bulletin board. Opposite the name Kitty Duval for our group, it said, "Karen Graham." The name Priscilla Teal was across from the words "A Society Lady." While I stood there considering tearing the paper into many small pieces, Julian came down the stairs and said, "Hello, P.T. Karen tells me you've taught her a brilliant American accent for Kitty." I couldn't think of anything to say for a minute. "Don't look so worried," he said, smiling. "I won't hold you responsible if she doesn't get it right. Not everyone's got your ear, you know. Now, as for you. I thought you might be interested in learning something about props. Nice period piece, that. Shall I put you down as props mistress?"

I stared at a green tack on the board for a moment, then said, "No. Absolutely not."

Julian opened his mouth, closed it, and then said, "Well. I see," and went into his office.

I left the building, instead of going to class. When I got to Karen's, she said, "Playing hooky? Good heavens, P.T., you are becoming bold. I hope it's not my rotten influence that's corrupting you." I sat on her floor all morning, weighing my options, while Karen lay on her side in bed, her head propped on one hand, reading the autobiography of a movie star. I could give up now and go home, I thought, or I could press doggedly on, getting odd little parts here and there until the year was over. Or I could do something drastic that would start events moving on an entirely different course. What would that be? I wondered.

In the early afternoon, Karen stood up to look in the mirror. "I'm positively revolting," she said, because her hair was dirty, and her nightie had become limp. "P.T.," she said, "draw me a bath, would you?"

The bathtub was in a tiny room down the hall. You had to put coins into a water heater to get it going. When the tub was full, Karen got in, and I took a clean nightgown and underpants from her top drawer. I brought these and a big saucepan into the bathroom, filled the pan from the tap, poured water over her hair, waited for her to lather it with shampoo, then filled the pan again and again to rinse all the bubbles away. "Thanks, P.T.," Karen said, leaning back against the tub. "I think I'll just lie here in my own muck for a few minutes, if you don't mind."

I went back to her room, changed the sheets, and straightened the clutter at the side of her bed. I had just picked up a mess of letters and candy wrappers when Karen's doorbell rang. Down the hall, between the inner and outer doors, John was leaning against the wall, pulling his boots off. It was raining. He was looking down at the boots when he said, "She didn't show up at school today, so I couldn't tell her not to come over. Sorry." Then he looked up with a beaming smile, recognized me, and let his face drop in disappointment. He said, "Where's Karen?"

"Taking a bath," I said. He followed me inside. I had a tearing feeling between my ribs, as if something were trapped there and trying to claw its way out.

"So Karen's playing Kitty Duval," he said, sitting down on a bag of dirty laundry at the foot of the bed. "Great role. What are you playing, P.T.? I forget."

"A very nice character part," I said. "You can learn a lot from those."

"I'll say." He nodded sincerely.

When Karen came back into the room, I had just finished straightening her letters and was reading the return address on the top one. She said, "P.T., what are you doing? Hello, John."

"Just cleaning up," I said.

She sat down on the corner of the bed. "Well, don't. I never suspected you had this appalling motherly streak. You shouldn't be so subservient. It puts people off. Hand me my comb, would you?" She dragged the comb through her wet tangles, then gave it back to me.

"You look better," John said. "Than I thought you would, I mean." He shifted his eyes nervously to check my reaction. He wasn't very convincing on stage, either.

"Thank you, John," Karen said, holding a strand of hair and examining it for split ends. "How nice of you to say so."

"Started on your lines, yet?" he said.

"Lines?" Karen turned to me. "Are the plays cast?"

John looked at me, too. "Didn't you tell her?"

"Not yet," I said.

John said, "You're playing Kitty Duval in *The Time of Your Life*, Karen."

"Well, bugger me," Karen said and coughed.

I said, "I have to go," and neither of them tried to talk me into staying. I didn't go straight home. I went to the same post office where, months before, I had called Eileen. In voice classs, we had been learning different kinds of English accents. The one I planned to use was Southern British Standard—SBS, our teacher, Alicia, called it. I chose the third red booth, though they were all empty. It was full of the cigarette smoke of a recent caller. I dialed the code for Australia, then the number for an operator. I said, "I'd like the number of Mr. Kevin Graham in Cowandilla, South Australia." She told me his number and then put the call through herself.

Kevin answered on the first ring. He sounded as though I had woke him up. I said, "This is a friend of Karen's. I'm phoning from England."

There was a slight delay while my voice traveled to Australia, he processed what I had just said, and his voice made its way back to me. He said, "Yes?" but he pronounced it "yiss?"

"I'm ringing to say that she is a little better today, and you can stop worrying."

Another pause. Then he said, "What? Has Karen been ill? Is she in hospital?"

"Oh, *dear*," I said. "You don't *know*. Perhaps it was a mistake to ring you at all, then. I am sorry. I suppose she wanted to prevent you from learning of her illness." My heart beat quickly now, and I felt a trickle of sweat roll from my armpit down the side of my rib cage.

Kevin said, "Holy fucking Christ."

"This is awful," I said. "She'd be positively livid if she knew I'd rung."

"Don't I know," he said, then added quickly, "but I won't tell her. I swear. Only, what is it that she's got?"

"That's one of the problems," I said. "All we know is that it's a nasty virus, and there's no known cure. But the cheering news is that she was able to sit up for quite a few minutes today and even had a little wash—with help, of course."

"My God," Kevin said.

"Now you must try and remember that she is going to get better. Well, it's practically certain."

"Jesus. What can I do?"

"Nothing. The only thing for her is a warm climate, but you know what England's like this time of year."

"Could I ring her? Can she speak to me?"

"Oh, she's lucid. There's even a phone. But, oh dear, this is awkward."

"You've got to give me the number."

"I'd like to, but then, you see, she'd know that I'd rung you. And I just don't like to upset her now that she's doing so well."

"I'll say I got it from her mum, for Christ's sake."

I said, "I'm really quite torn." Once I had the vowels and the intonation right, this perfectly authentic phrase came out spontaneously.

He said, "She's my *wife*."

"Yes, of course," I said. "I suppose you do have a point. All right." I gave him the number, then repeated it. He thanked me and started to ask me something else about Karen's symptoms. I said, "I'm sorry, I can't quite hear you. Sorry? Hello? Hello?" Then I shouted, "I'm ringing off now!" and hung up on him. I went to the counter and paid for my call.

There is a rule for an effective performance that is pretty obvious, really, but hard to remember, especially when a show is going well. The rule is always keep your audience wanting more.

At home, I wrote a couple of letters, read a little while, and went to bed. Even though it was well after nine, I left my heater on. I didn't turn it off all night. It had just dawned on me that I could have it on round the clock, and no one would ever know.

After school the next day, I went to Karen's, as usual. She was out of bed, dressed, and hurling her belongings into boxes and suitcases. "Are you moving?" I said.

"No. Leaving."

"What do you mean?"

"Kevin has rung me. He wants me to come home, and I'm going."

"What?" I said. "He called?" I opened my mouth wide and left it that way for a few beats as I sat down on the bed. "You're leaving school?"

"Right," said Karen. "Now, what have I done with my passport? Well, it's in here somewhere, I reckon."

"But your part," I said. "You've got another good part this time."

"You think I'd stay here for a *part*?" Karen said.

I said, "I would. I'd give up almost anything for a good part."

"Your devotion is inspirational," she said. "Come on, P.T. The school isn't exactly top-notch, is it? I mean, the director drinks, the dance instructor is crazy as a snake, and I mastered all the bloody tongue exercises for voice class in about five minutes. It's all very well trotting off to England to do some classes, live in a shabby bed-sit, buy cutlery off the street, and all that. But it's not real life, is it?" She picked up the lamp shade she had bought on Portobello Road, then squashed it into a box of garbage. I watched her cram several books into the suitcase, then try to shut it over a tremendous bulge of stuff. Finally, she sat down hard on the lid and snapped it shut. "You're a big help," she said. Then she started grabbing dresses and blouses off their hangers in the closet and stuffing them into another bag.

"Do you have to leave right away?" I said. "What's the big emergency? Can't you wait a few days?"

"Are you joking? I'd go mad. What if he changed his mind?"

"I thought you said you were off men. If he changes his mind that fast, I don't know why you're going back."

She straightened up and fixed me with a cold stare. Then she said coolly, "You are very näive, P.T."

"Well," I said. "If you really think this is going to make you happy, I guess you should go."

"Thanks so much," she said.

We didn't talk anymore for the next half hour, while Karen continued packing. When she was nearly finished, she took three cardboard boxes out to the garbage cans, put tape and her Australian address on two others, and stood her suitcases side by side in front of her emptied dresser.

"I'll go to the airport with you," I said. "I can help you carry your things."

"Good," she said. "What a terrific mate."

There was a stop for the bus to Heathrow a couple of blocks from Karen's place. I had the heaviest of the two suitcases and hung the carry-on bag over my shoulder. I had to hold the handle of the suitcase with both hands, letting it bang painfully against my knees. As we waited for the bus, I said, "Karen, are you sure they're going to let you take all this? It must be way over the weight limit."

"Not to worry," she said. "As you know, I can get away with anything." On the bus, we had to ask two Dutch boys with backpacks to hoist the suitcases into the rack.

At the check-in counter, the ticket agent said the bags were overweight. "There's an extra-baggage fee," she said. Karen drew herself up into a straight line and pursed her lips, indignant. Even with all our money pooled, we didn't have enough to cover it.

Leaving both suitcases on the scale, Karen opened one and pulled a layer of clothes, books, and tins of candy off the top. These she handed to me, item by item, checking the reading on the scale each time. When she had gotten her load down to an acceptable weight, she snapped the bag shut, looked at me holding all her things, took the black bowler off her head, and put it on mine. "It suits you," she said. The ticket agent shuffled her papers impatiently. "Carry on," Karen told her. She sniffed, assigned Karen an aisle seat, and handed back the ticket. "Thank you for your infinite kindness, madam," Karen said loudly.

I walked with her as far as the security check to say good-bye. "Well, P.T.," she said, "have a lovely time here in England, if that's possible. Personally, I can't wait to see it as a small gray patch miles beneath me." She shifted her shoulder bag. Then she said, "There's something you should know." For a second I thought she was going to tell me about her affair with John. She said, "You're very good. As an actress, I mean. You're like this sort of blank cassette tape, ready to pick up all the voices in the air." She waved a hand around. "Or a dry sponge soaking up every odd little fleck of personality it wipes across. Or you're this kind of clear soup stock, taking on a different flavor, depending on what old bones and vegetables of character somebody bungs into you. You're like . . ." She paused and tilted her face up at the monitor that displayed flight times and gate numbers. "Well, I can't think of anything else empty enough. You just seem to become all these different people, which is rather good, if you see what I mean. If you're serious about this, you ought to go to New York." She looked at her watch. "Right. I'm off. Cheers."

I had to put the messy pile I was holding down on the floor in order to hug her. "Good luck," I said, "I hope it works out with Kevin."

"Goodbye, P.T.," said Karen. She turned to push her bag into the X-ray machine and walk through the metal detector. Then she made her way down a long corridor in the direction of her gate. When she got to the end of the hall, Karen turned around to wave at me. The move was confident; without looking, she knew that I would still be standing there, my arms around her belongings, watching her walk away. By the time she disappeared around a corner, I was crying and had to put everything down again to wipe my nose on a pair of Karen's dance tights.

Before I got back on the bus, I bought a plastic bag to put all Karen's things in. Not everything fit, so I draped an enormous purple shawl around the shoulders of my coat.

I was walking from the bus to the Hoddings-Leighs' when I ran into Julian James and his wife, Felicity. They were holding hands. In their other hands, they were holding newspaper bundles of fish and chips. I said, "Julian, I have to tell you something."

He looked startled for a moment, then peered at me closely. "Oh, P.T.," he said. "It's you. Heavens. You're looking rather self-possessed. Whatever have you done?"

"I guess it's the hat," I said. "Anyway, Karen had to go back to Australia. Family emergency. I'm supposed to tell you that she won't be returning to finish the year."

"Won't be paying the school fees she owes, either, I suppose," said Felicity.

"Oh," I said. "She didn't mention that."

"Well," said Julian. "All right." He started to walk away.

"One more thing," I said. "I want to play Kitty Duval. I know all the lines already."

Julian chortled. "I see. You've got rid of Karen via some underhanded plot. A few mysterious, untraceable drops in her teacup, was it?" Even Felicity smiled. "Why, you may have her hacked-up remains in that innocent-looking carry bag."

"Oh, poor P.T.," said Felicity. "Stop it, Julian. You've made her look quite guilty. Give her the part and shut up."

"Yes," Julian said. "Our chips are getting cold. You may play Kitty."

I said, "Thank you," but he didn't hear me. The two of them had turned away and were hurrying home to eat their fish and chips.

As Kitty Duval, my main difficulty was learning to speak in my own voice and not adopting any odd mannerisms. I wasn't used to playing straight roles. I got the hang of it quickly enough, though, and particularly enjoyed the performances and having streams of words come out without interruption and looking out into a whole roomful of people with their eyes trained on me. The parts I played after that were all people around my own age—ingenues. These weren't as challenging as the character roles had been, but they were larger and I got more attention and credit for doing them.

Once I had returned from London, I never heard from Karen, which is only logical, as she wasn't there during the second term, when I told everyone my real name. John stayed in England after school ended. He decided he was not a good actor, after all, and Julian hired him to teach character development and scene study at The Theatre School. Six months after their wedding, Matthew and Harriet were talking about children, and I moved to New York to begin acting professionally.

ESP Experiments

My sister died; I was going to have a baby. These were my first two thoughts every morning. The day of our last childbirth-preparation class, I woke up clutching a jar of Tums. Someone in the class had told me that to get labor started when a baby was overdue you should eat a hot, spicy meal. The night before, my husband, Tom, and I had gone to a Mexican restaurant. The night before that, we tried an Indian place. Before that, we ate Italian food at a restaurant with garlic bread so strong it made your eyes water. All I got was heartburn.

Now, as we lay in bed, Tom had his hands against my big belly. "How are you feeling?" he said.

"Fat," I said. "But all right."

Tom was feeling the baby thrashing around inside me, a daily ritual for about the past four months. "I think little Zelda is going to be good at sports," he said. We knew we were having a girl and referred to her as little Zelda because we hadn't thought of a name yet.

I said, "I just hope she doesn't get much bigger. Pretty soon she's going to be kicking me in the chin." I sat up, then rested before standing, which I knew was going to take some effort. I said, "Maybe if I had a talk with her, she'd be born soon. I could tell her how nice her room looks and about all the toys we bought. They say babies recognize their mothers' voices, even this early."

Tom said, "Talk to her? You mean the way people talk to plants? Oh, Jenny." He laughed and got up to take a shower.

I went to the kitchen to make coffee and pour some raisin bran in a bowl for him. A little while later, Tom came in tying his tie. "How are you feeling?" he said.

"You already asked me. I'm still fine. When you're pregnant," I said, "people don't say, 'How are you?' the way they do to everyone else. They say, 'How are you feeling?'" I took a pinch of the dry cereal and put it in my mouth. "I'm not myself," I said. "The waiting is getting to me." I took another pinch, making sure I got a raisin this time.

Tom took the bowl from me and poured milk into it. "Well, it won't be long now," he said.

"If one more person says that," I said, "I'm not going to have this baby. I'm just going to hold it in forever."

"Jesus," Tom said. "Do you have to be like this all the time? Everyone is just trying to be nice." He shook his head. Then he ate his cereal, rinsed the bowl, and left it in the sink. "I'll see you tonight," he said and left.

I went to the baby's room, sank down in the rocking chair with the pink-and-white cushions I had made myself. I had finished off my last free-lance assignment—writing the text of annual reports, brochures, and pamphlets for a public relations company—the week before. The weather was awful—freezing rain—so I would stay home and try to find things to do, pretending I was not just waiting for this baby to be born. I turned on a cassette I had already loaded into the tape player near the crib. The tape was for soothing a fussy baby to sleep. It was a recording of the intrauterine sounds of a woman eight-and-a-half months pregnant. In an article I read, a pediatrician said that no new parent should be without it, so I sent away for it. I leaned my head against the rocker and closed my eyes.

Tom and I were having a hard time. Part of it had to do with my sister dying. It was an accident. Alison was hit by a car the year before while riding her bicycle near her apartment in Denver. We had gotten through the first few months well enough, the time when I was crying all the time and didn't want to go anywhere or talk. But then I went through a phase of talking a lot about Alison, and that was when this empty hole opened up between us.

I didn't feel that Tom had ever understood about my sister and me, so I thought of stories to tell him to show how close we had been as kids. I saved them to tell in bed at night or on long car trips or in restaurants while we were waiting for our food. On the way home from a wedding in Stockbridge, I told him about the times Alison and I had laughed in church. I said, "It began with a snicker from one of us that would set the other off instantly. We didn't even have to know what the joke was. Pretty soon, we were both holding our noses, heads bowed, shoulders shaking, praying that we would not guffaw or snort out loud. Once we got this far, no amount of cheek-biting or arm-pinching could stop us. Our parents would pretend not to notice for as long as they could, then one of them would glare and point to the parking lot. Alison and I would slip out the side exit."

Tom didn't get what I was trying to say. "You guys went to church?" he said. "I didn't know that."

"For a while. But I mean, even without speaking, we would both start giggling out of control." I snapped my fingers. "Like that." Tom nodded slowly.

On a friend's futon on Cape Cod one weekend, I whispered another story to Tom. "Once our neighbors down the street put up a platform swing," I said. "You had to stand on this wooden ledge on a steep hill, holding the rope of the swing, then jump off, and in midair bring your legs around the rope, lowering your behind onto a skinny board. Alison just climbed up the ladder, grabbed the rope, and jumped. She wasn't afraid of anything. But I went up and just stood there for ages. I'd bend my knees as if I was about to take off and then look down and chicken out. The other kids yelled at me to hurry, while Alison mimed the way I was to hold the rope and push off with my legs. Then she began a countdown: 'Five, four, three, two, one. Jump!' And I did. I kept my eyes closed and trusted her confidence that I was not going to kill myself."

Tom said, "Some people are more athletic than others."

"Sure, but I mean I could do things I wouldn't ordinarily try because I had Alison. We had this kind of telepathic connection."

I told him about our ESP experiments. "Lying in bed at night," I said, "one of us would picture an object, while the other tried to guess what it was. The trick was to sort of mentally breathe her in. Then her thought would suddenly appear in my head: a flat tire, a guitar, a beach towel. She could read my mind, too. She always gave her answer quickly before she had a chance to think about it." Telling Tom about it, I could almost feel those nights exactly as they had been. Alison and I would be wide awake in our room, the taste of Crest in our mouths. I could almost hear her whisper, "A burning house!" across the dark space separating our beds. And between us, the air seemed hot, charged, crackling. "Yes!" I could hear myself say.

"Look," Tom said. "I don't think you should make too much of that kind of thing. Childhood memories are very unreliable. And you were sisters growing up in the same house, sharing a bedroom. It's not so strange that you had similar ideas." Tom majored in psychology. "She was your older sister, and you convinced yourself that she had supernatural powers."

This was the way Tom disappointed me. He only saw certain parts of Alison. To him, she was a fourth-grade teacher with red hair to her waist many years after long hair was fashionable, whose only long-term relationships had been with a married man, who eventually dumped her, and her two cats. The fact that Alison didn't drive stood out in Tom's mind more than the qualities that I tried to show him. I pointed out her sense of humor, her energy, and her powerful presence. Sometimes after several rounds of ESP experiments, Alison would fall asleep. I knew that she was sleeping, even before I whispered her name and got no reply, because the atmosphere changed. The air lost its charge, went flat. Since she died, I felt as if a vital part of me had been unplugged.

I stopped trying to talk about Alison, and Tom began to go out more by himself. He played basketball in the park on Saturdays and at the gym a couple of evenings a week. When there was a Boston Celtics game on television, he stayed home. But then he was unreachable, even during the commercials, when he gave angry speeches about what the team was doing wrong. Larry Bird was out the whole season, and they kept losing. Meanwhile Tom was having his own streak of bad luck. He sold real estate in Cambridge, and the market was in a slump. Soon after we bought our own condo with skylights in the kitchen and bathroom, a woodburning stove, and hardwood floors, the real-estate boom began to reverse itself. Now he had stopped talking about his work. Maybe he thought it would upset me too much to know how badly things were going; maybe he thought it would be bad for me now to worry. I didn't know what he thought, and I was lonely.

When I got pregnant, I tried to focus on the baby's coming. I bought several books on pregnancy and the birthing process and a few more about babies. I made sure that we had all the right baby equipment far ahead of time. I didn't want anything to go wrong. I didn't want to be surprised.

Now I sat up straighter in the rocking chair and practiced the breathing exercises we had learned in childbirth class. Then I lowered myself to the floor and did my daily routine of exercises for toning and stretching the muscles I would use during the birth. Finally, for fifteen minutes, I sat in a squatting position while reading a pamphlet on breastfeeding. When I had finished all this, I pushed the stop button on the baby's tape player and rewound the sleep cassette. I had paid eleven dollars for it, including shipping and handling. It sounded like a dishwasher.

Tom and I sat down in Room 310 of CHMC—Cambridge Health Maintenance Center—for our childbirth class. Miriam, our teacher, was dragging a table to the center of the room for the food we were all supposed to bring because this was our last meeting. Miriam was a nurse-practitioner downstairs in OB-GYN. She had short, wiry gray hair and wore bright clothes and big silver earrings. Usually at this time she set up charts showing cervical dilation and the types of breathing appropriate for each stage of labor. But tonight there would be only a short review and then a video of a birth. She left the room and returned a minute later, pushing a television and a VCR on a cart.

Laura and Mark came in. Laura carried a plate of fudge to the table. I walked over to put down the chocolate-chip cookies I had brought and took a piece of fudge. "I wasn't going to eat tonight," I said. "And look at me."

"Stop it," Laura said. "You haven't gained anything. Your arms and legs are sticks. What have you put on—ten or twelve pounds? I'm a whale."

"You look adorable," I said. "And I've gained twenty-seven pounds. Does that make you feel better?" Tom looked at Laura's husband, who shook his head. "O.K.," I said, putting a hand to my side where my hip used to be. "I'd like to see you guys swell up like blimps, and see how you'd handle it."

Teresa and Robin joined us at the food table. Robin had brought macaroons. Teresa opened a bag of cheese-covered popcorn. "All natural," she said, smoothing a napkin across the top of her big stomach. She took one of each kind of sweet and placed them on the napkin.

Miriam said, "O.K., let's get this show on the road. Take some food and sit." She clapped her hands twice and we stopped talking and went back to our seats. She tugged her purple turtleneck down over her jeans and looked at an index card she was holding. "We have a baby." We all looked around to see who was missing. "Scott and Andrea had a baby girl named Hilary. She was born last Wednesday at six-thirty-four. Nine pounds, eight ounces."

I swallowed. "Cesarean?"

"Nope," Miriam said.

Laura whispered, "Oh my God." She put her hand over her mouth. "The poor woman." Across the room, Teresa covered her eyes. A piece of fudge fell off her stomach and rolled under a chair.

"All right," Miriam said. "A little reminder: Childbirth *hurts*. Anyone who says labor feels like menstrual cramps is—" she cupped her hand around her ear and leaned into the class. "*What?*" she said, prompting us.

"*Childless, a man, or lying!*" we all chanted in chorus.

"Thank you. Now. I see those lips moving, but let's solidify a few points. Drugs. Moms, I do not want to hear any stories of heroics when you call to tell me about your deliveries."

She pointed her finger and made a sweep with it around the room, eyeballing each woman in turn. "I mean it now, moms. Let's be *flexible!* If you think you'd be better off with a little medical intervention, *ask* for it. Everybody with me here? Good! By the same token, moms, let's not walk into that hospital demanding to be knocked out. You may be capable of more than you think." She paused to watch us nod. "Remember your breathing. Everyone is practicing on a *daily* basis, I hope. And when you get in there, *use* it! All right. Dads. What's your role?"

Matthew, Harriet's husband, said, "To be her advocate." They were having twins.

"That's right, dads. *Listen* to mom. During active labor, she may not be very articulate. Talk to the doctor for her, get that nurse when she needs something. You know her better than anybody." I wondered if the other couples in the class were really practicing the breathing exercises together. In the morning Tom was always in a hurry, and at night he seemed so tired. I was afraid that we were not close enough now for him to help me during the delivery the way the husbands were supposed to. I was afraid that I would try to tell him something, and he would not know what I meant.

Miriam said, "Now, let's quit yakking and see this movie." She shoved a videotape into the VCR, pushed some buttons, and turned on the television. As the music for the video started, she switched off the lights in the room. We watched a couple arrive at the hospital to have their baby. As they walked down the hall to their room, the woman stopped to grip a doorknob and grimace. Her husband rubbed her back as she hunched over, exhaling loudly. She rocked back and forth, closed her eyes, inhaled deeply, and groaned. We watched them advance through the stages of labor. A clock appeared every now and then to show how much time had elapsed. After seven hours, the doctor was with them and the woman was pushing. The camera took the doctor's perspective. I took a number of deep breaths and let them out slowly. Several times the baby seemed about to be born, but it kept sliding back. There was blood; the woman screamed.

I started thinking about my sister's accident. I couldn't help it. It happened at night on a busy street four blocks from her apartment. She was probably just going to get some ice cream—she was crazy about Häagen-Dazs. She wasn't wearing her bicycle helmet. No one saw the car that hit her, not the license number, the make, or even the color. Many times, I had tried to picture the way it happened, but it never came out the same way twice. Once I imagined that a Mercedes hit her while making an illegal U-turn. The car was stolen, so the driver was afraid to stop. Another time, the car was an old Ford station wagon. Alison swerved left to avoid a pothole just as the driver weaved right. He was drunk. Tonight I pictured a speeding Mustang full of laughing teenagers, passing a slow truck on the right just as Alison moved into the same lane to turn left. I saw my sister lying near a curb with her eyes closed.

My sister died just as she was coming out of a long depression. She and her boyfriend had split up. Maybe this sad period had started earlier and I hadn't noticed. In any case, she became reclusive and disorganized. She stopped doing the things she enjoyed, like riding her bike and traveling. Her Christmas presents to us arrived in February or March with rambling, apologetic notes. My mother said her apartment was a mess. Clothes, dirty dishes, and cat hair were all over the place. I tried to get her to come to Cambridge to stay with us for a while. She wouldn't. My parents gave her the names of three therapists in her area, but this only made her angry.

All of a sudden, the last eight or so months before she died, she was a lot better. I went out to visit her during the summer. Her apartment was immaculate, and she had started taking long bike rides again on weekends. She had given her cats away to two fourth graders in her class, because she said she was sick of being tied down. We played miniature golf at a place near her apartment and got laughing so hard that we could barely hit the ball. When it was time for me to fly home, I didn't want to leave.

A few months later, Alison was dead. Returning from the funeral, Tom and I found a package outside our door. Our Christmas presents from Alison: a calendar with closeup photographs of kitchen herbs for each month, a scarf and hat for Tom, a silver bangle tied in a square knot for me. My parents got a package, too: a cotton cable-stitch cardigan for my mother and a hardcover spy novel for my father. Alison had already done her Christmas shopping and been to the post office by early December.

In the movie, the baby was born. It was a boy. The whole business was a lot more gory than I expected, and I felt the blood drain from my head as the doctor handed the baby to his mother. I leaned against Tom. The music came on again. Miriam turned on the lights. A lot of the women were crying, including Laura, who asked me for a tissue. I dug around in my purse and gave her a little pack.

Miriam wiped away tears with her hand. "I must have seen that thing thirty times, and it always gets to me. Let's take a break."

I was standing with the other women at the food table when Scott and Andrea walked in. We all crowded around them to see their new baby. Andrea was holding her, wrapped in a pink blanket. Miriam said, "Welcome to the world,

Hilary! Andrea, take a seat." Miriam held the baby, while Scott and Andrea took their coats off.

"O.K., dads," Scott said. He pulled a six-pack of Grolsch beer out of a paper bag and carried it to the food table. "It's Miller time."

The men followed him to the food table. I heard Tom say, "Congratulations."

Scott shook his head and said, "What a week."

I waited until all the other women had finished, then I went over to see the baby. With one finger, Andrea pulled the blanket away from Hilary's face. Hilary stared cross-eyed at a fold in the blanket. There was a blister in the center of her top lip from nursing, and she had a lot of tiny pimples across her cheeks and nose. Her head looked pointed, and she was practically bald. I said, "She's beautiful."

"I know," Andrea said. "I can't believe how perfect she is."

I sat down next to Andrea. I said, "I'm scared." But Andrea didn't hear me because the baby suddenly opened her mouth and started to cry. Her whole head turned scarlet and her body arched. Her arms flailed, loosening her blanket until a flap of it slid off.

Andrea said, "Here we go. Hold her for me, will you?" She handed the baby to me and started rummaging around under her sweater. I looked down at Hilary, eyes shut tight, mouth open wide, gulping in air between howls. She felt hard under the blanket, not soft and cuddly the way I expected, but tough and wiry. Her heels thumped against my stomach, causing my own baby to flip and twist in response. Andrea's cried harder. The people in the class looked at me, as if I were the cause, as if I should make her stop. "Shh," I said and started swaying back and forth. "Is this right?" I said to Andrea.

"I have no idea," she said. She took Hilary and gave her a breast under her sweater. The room was quiet for a few seconds before conversations began again. I said to Andrea, "We just saw a film of a birth. How was your delivery?"

She groaned. "They say you forget all about it by the time you're ready to have the next one," she said. "I can't wait."

I put a hand over my stomach. "What was so bad about it?"

"The pain."

"Oh," I said. I looked down at the baby, whose whole being was concentrated on nursing. Her tiny hand gripped Andrea's sweater, her eyes were slits, and she made little grunting sounds as she sucked. I said, "Well, anyway, congratulations. She's gorgeous."

I sat down next to Tom again. Brushing my bangs off my forehead, I found that my face was damp with sweat. One last time, Miriam reviewed the stages of labor and the types of breathing that went with each. Then she gave us each a little card with her phone number on it. "I want to hear from everyone within forty-eight hours of the birth," she said. "Well, that's it. Best of luck to all of you." We all wished each other good luck.

I drove home because Tom had had a beer in class. As I turned onto Inman Street, a cat streaked out from between two parked cars. Listening to the tires screech against the pavement, I thought, There is no way we're going to stop in time; I am going to run over it. But I had always been a poor judge of distance. The car stopped a few feet from the cat. For a moment, it froze in the middle of the street, its eyes reflecting the car's headlights back at Tom and me, then it dashed off onto the porch railing of a two-family house. From there the cat leaped onto the top of a shutter. A woman opened the front door. "Wonton?" she said. "Here, kitty, kitty."

I could feel my heart pounding. "Oh, God," I said. "I almost hit it."

Tom said, "Are you O.K.?"

"Yeah, fine."

"Are you sure? Jen, you're shaking. Pull over behind that van."

I parked the car. I looked at the cat again. The woman was patting her thighs, speaking softly to the cat, urging him to come down. His paws were clustered under him on the narrow shutter. "Come on, Wonton, baby," she said. The cat didn't budge. She kept trying, going to the door, as if about to abandon him up there; whistling; and making kissing sounds. Wonton stayed on the shutter, mewing anxiously and craning his neck toward the ground. The woman gave up and went inside.

I put my hands over my face and said, "I'm so scared. That movie. I don't think I can do it."

"Sure you can, honey," Tom said. "It won't be as bad as you think."

"How do you know? You can't be positive of that. It might be worse. If it gets really awful," I said, "make them give me drugs. *Make* them."

"They're not going to let you suffer," Tom said. "I'm sure if you need medication, the doctor will know it."

"But what if they expect me to tolerate more pain than I can? And don't let them give me a cesarean. No matter what."

"I can't promise that, Jen. It might be necessary. Three out of ten, Miriam said."

"You're not the one who has to live through it, Tom. I do not want a cesarean."

"Jennifer, it's not going to be my decision."

"Can't you reassure me a little? Even if it's not true, can't you just say that, no matter what happens, you won't let anything bad happen to me? Just to make me feel better?" Tom took a deep breath. "Once we're at the hospital, don't leave me alone, O.K.?"

"Of course I won't."

"Good." The baby rearranged herself, kicking me in the ribs. "O.K., thanks."

Tom said, "We might have to sell the condo."

"What?"

"I'm not making enough money." He looked out the window. "Without your checks, it's really going to be hard. Just when we need the space and the security of owning something. I don't know if I can make the payments. Already the baby is so expensive. I just didn't know all the equipment was going to cost so much."

"Oh," I said. "Let's move then."

"I don't think you understand," he said. "The value of the place has really dropped. We won't make anywhere near the profit we thought we would. We might even lose money on it."

"That's too bad."

Tom said, "You don't even care, do you?"

"Yes, I do," I said. "I just don't care as much as you do."

"Well, what about the baby?"

I said, "I can't speak for the baby, of course. But I think she's going to care even less than I do about giving up a skylight in the bathroom and hardwood floors. Maybe we could buy something cheap in a cruddy neighborhood. Maybe we could rent for a while. Or maybe the whole thing will work out better than you think."

"Oh, sure. That's right. Maybe the whole problem will

magically evaporate." Tom shook his head and sighed, meaning that I didn't know the first thing about real estate.

The cat woman came outside again, and the two of us watched her for a while. Wonton still hadn't come down from the shutter. There was something so familiar about this scene. I watched a moment longer until it hit me what it was: Alison coaxing me onto the platform swing.

"My sister," I said. "I've been thinking about the last time I saw her, about the way she had everything in her apartment so perfectly organized. She had given away all her old clothes so her closets had enough room for everything to hang freely, so the hangers slid easily back and forth on the pole. In her bedroom, all the dresses were on the left, then the blouses, then pants. The shoes were arranged in groups according to style—dressy, casual, and sport. All her life Alison had dumped her clothes on a chair at the end of the day. On the refrigerator were lists of places she wanted to ride her bike to during the summer, places she wanted to see. She had gotten her hair cut short, as if she wanted to blend in, to disappear. I'm thinking about the way she found homes for those cats. And remember how the Christmas presents arrived so far ahead of time?" Tom looked at me. "It wasn't an accident," I said. "She was depressed and covering it up. She rode in front of that car on purpose. It wasn't an accident at all. She planned to die and got herself organized for it."

"Oh, God," Tom said quietly. We sat there not speaking for a few minutes, sleet melting against the car and dripping down the windshield as traffic slid by. I started the car again and drove home. I was pulling up on the emergency brake when I felt something hurt me hard from inside. It started below the base of my spine and fanned out across my lower back. It was a grinding pain, rather than a cramp. I caught my breath, about to cry out—not because of the pain but from the recognition of what it was—but then it was gone. Walking to the house, I stepped carefully over patches of snow and ice.

At the hospital, I was wearing a flimsy gown and my socks. Patty, our nurse, held my hand while I walked in a small circle next to the bed. Tom held my other hand, leaning over to see my face. I breathed in through my nose and slowly out through my mouth. Tom and Patty did it with me. This was the routine we had developed in the hour or so since we had checked into the hospital. We were still waiting for the doctor to come and examine me. When the contraction ended, Tom said, "All *right*, Jen. You're golden," the way I imagined he would if I had skyhooked a basketball. Then he helped me back to the bed. Patty handed me a cup of ice chips. I was thirsty, and the hospital didn't allow laboring women to drink anything, in case there was a need for anesthesia.

A man came in. "I'm Dr. Comstock," he said. "I'm on call tonight for CHMC. Let's take a look." He said this to Tom. Then he examined me while gazing at the wall behind my head, as if there were something fascinating stuck to it. I knew this doctor. I had seen him once when my own was on vacation. I thought he was condescending.

Now I gasped and said, "Stop. You're hurting me."

But he was finished. He said, "Five centimeters. Her first, right? She's got a long way to go. I'm going to try to get some sleep." He wasn't talking to me or Tom now but to Patty, the nurse. He headed for the door.

I said, "Excuse me. If it gets really bad, may I have something for pain?"

He poked his head back around the door and said, "Why don't you try to be a big girl and see how things go? We don't want to make this any slower than it has to be." Then he was gone.

I turned to Tom. I wanted to say, "Did you hear that? He told me to be a big girl." But I didn't want to hear Tom say that we knew before we joined our health plan that we would have no control over who delivered our baby.

Another contraction started, and I breathed with Tom. Then they began to come after shorter pauses. Tom switched us to a different kind of breathing—hee, hee, hee, ha, instead of slow chest breathing. I said to Patty, "Are you sure it's going to be a long time?"

She said, "Do the contractions feel a lot stronger now?" I nodded. "Then you're probably going to be quicker than Dr. Comstock thought. Labor can be unpredictable." Patty called someone to bring more ice chips for me and a ginger ale for Tom.

Soon the contractions were so strong and frequent that Patty and Tom became like ghosts: I noticed the disturbance they made but couldn't quite perceive them. I was tearing in half. I didn't get up now but stayed on the bed, sometimes gripping one of them by an arm or shirt. It was so hot. Patty pinned my hair back off my face. Tom used a wet cloth to cool me. As soon as my skin warmed it, the cloth felt disgusting, and I shook my head to get it off. Patty held a metal pan for me to vomit into.

A resident came in to examine me. She was young and had a Caribbean accent and cool, gentle hands. "I'm Mary Percy. You've been working hard, Jenny," she said. "You're fully dilated. You can start pushing. First tell me how you're doing."

"Thirsty," I said. "Hot."

"I'm so sorry," she said and came to stand next to me. I

took her cool, brown hand and held it against my face. I didn't feel embarrassed doing this; I didn't even try to stop myself. She smelled of coffee and soap and let me lean on her for a minute or so, then smoothed my hair and started out. "I'll check on you later," she said.

I said, "Wait," but she was gone.

"Ha, ha, ha," Tom and Patty breathed at me through the next contraction. I couldn't look at them. Now it hurt too much to try anything so idiotic. Patty said, "Don't get discouraged now. You're getting there." Tom wiped my face with the cloth.

During the next group of contractions, Tom took one leg and Patty took the other, shoving them up near my shoulders, while I pushed. They shouted encouraging things to me: "Come on. Atta girl! Push, push, push, push. Yes!" In between pushes, I closed my eyes and left the room, only to open them again, surprised to find myself in a hospital, having a baby. Once I wanted to announce that I couldn't do it anymore, but I was too exhausted to move my mouth. Then Patty said, "Jenny, I see the baby's head! Tom, look! There's your baby!"

Tom's tired face lit up. "I can see her, Jen. Our baby!" His hand shook with excitement as he held my leg.

Wanting so badly for this to be over, I had forgotten there was a baby in there. When I started to push harder, Tom and Patty yelled at me about what a great job I was doing. They didn't know anything. I wasn't doing it; I didn't have any influence over the process anymore. There was just this baby, stronger than any of us, struggling to get free of me, even if it meant ripping me to pieces.

Suddenly Patty walked to my side and said sharply, "Listen to me. Don't push now. Hear me? Don't push. Tom, get her to pant."

Tom puffed out little short breaths and I tried to imitate

him. I squeezed his wrist, and he whispered, "Almost. Almost, Jenny."

Patty walked quickly to the phone. "Dr. Comstock, Room 4, please," she said. "Room 4. Dr. Comstock." She checked me again while we waited. "Hang on," she said. "Just a minute more, Jenny." Then she went back to the phone and said, more urgently this time, "Dr. Comstock to Room 4, please. Dr. Comstock. Room 4."

Tom was panting all by himself now. I bit my lip. The baby was trying to get out. I said, "I have to push. I have to."

"O.K., Jenny," Patty said. She ran to the telephone. She said, "Any doctor to Room 4. Any doctor." I could hear her voice both beside me and over the intercom out in the hall. The room filled with people.

Dr. Percy reached me first, and I began to push with everything I had. Her cool hands were on my thighs. "Jenny," she said. "I need to make a cut to help the baby out. We'll give you a local anesthetic."

I said, "Hurry."

Dr. Percy and another woman were busy for a few seconds. The other woman was Alison. I saw a strand of her red hair hanging out of her green cap. She was busy unwrapping sterile supplies and placing them on a tray, pushing the paper wrappers aside as she worked. Dr. Percy was holding a needle when Dr. Comstock walked in. "I'll take over now," he said.

I looked at Tom and heard myself say, "Help," but I couldn't manage to tell him what I wanted.

Tom turned to Dr. Comstock and said, "Thank you, but we'd like Dr. Percy to deliver the baby."

"I'm the CHMC doctor on call tonight," Dr. Comstock said. "I'm your wife's doctor."

"No," Tom said. "I'm sorry. We want Dr. Percy. That's our decision."

Dr. Comstock said, "It's hospital policy—"

Tom took a step toward Dr. Comstock. At the same moment, Alison fell in behind him, as if to back him up, as if the two of them had something planned. Or this was the way it appeared to me. Another contraction started. I closed my eyes. When I opened them, Dr. Comstock was gone.

Dr. Percy was shouting, "Jenny, we have the baby's head! Now let's get the shoulders." The shoulders took three pushes. Then there was a slippery whooshing feeling and Patty, grinning, handed the baby to me. She was blue and bloody but warm, almost hot, which felt nice, as I was freezing now. The baby was studying me. Her lips were puckered and she was peering down her nose at me, looking prim and regal at the same time. "Victoria," I said. "Could we call her Victoria?"

"Yeah," Tom said. "Victoria." He climbed up on the bed beside me, kissing my neck.

I am in bed, holding the baby, who is asleep. We are going home this afternoon. I just took a shower and my hair has left two wet spots on the shoulders of the new pink nightgown that Tom gave me. My grandmother sent flowers, pink roses and baby's breath, and Tom is filling a vase with water from the bathroom. He is whistling "Old MacDonald Had a Farm." Tom says that Victoria's arrival has changed everything. First the Celtics won a game last night. Then this morning a client of his made an offer on an expensive three-family house. I feel the change, too. I am excited and happy, as though I've found something precious—a favorite ring or necklace—that I thought was lost forever.

I examine the baby again. There are tiny veins on her eyelids, and she has long, dark lashes. One of her little hands has come out of the receiving blanket that the nurse has wound tightly around her and is up near her face, clenched in a tight fist. I pull the blanket away and look at her ear. It's too small. I uncurl her fingers and look at them. Tom comes out of the bathroom and bends down to see what I am staring at. For a moment, I know what Tom is thinking. Without looking at him, I know he knows what I'm thinking, too. I am sure of it. We are thinking, She even has fingernails. Perfect.

Celia

I had lived only a short distance from Celia for four years, but I never expected to see her again. Celia was my ex-husband's daughter by his first wife. To my amazement, one day she called me from a booth in Harvard Square to say she wanted to come over. I said, "I'd love to see you," and told her how to get to my place. Then I ran around sweeping the baby's crackers off the kitchen floor, putting away the sandals I had left under the coffee table, and straightening the bath-room towels.

I hadn't seen Celia in five years, since she was eleven and her father and I rented a house for a week near the beach in Summerland outside of Santa Barbara. Just that one week's rent cost as much as a month in our apartment in Los Angeles, but it was worth it, we said, if Celia had a good time and got to know her father better. Or I guess I was the one who said this; I don't think Richard was that optimistic.

Celia did not have a good time. She refused to swim in the pool that glittered expensively in the perfect weather. Instead she sat outside, wearing a pair of thick corduroys and a white sweatshirt with padded shoulders, putting on and taking off fingernail polish, leafing through her scrapbook of Princess Diana clippings. She called her mother every day.

When Richard tried to stop all the long-distance phoning, I wouldn't let him. This was Celia's first extended visit with us, and I didn't want her to be unhappy. She kept asking for things like Cheetos, and I made special trips to the store. The meals I cooked were not acceptable to her. Once I made soup with mushrooms and heavy cream; a broccoli frittata another time; and one morning for breakfast, whole-wheat pancakes with a choice of powdered sugar or maple syrup. Celia would say, "Yuck, Laura. What *is* this?" Finally, I just boiled some macaroni and dumped warmed-up canned spaghetti sauce over it. She said, "Noodles? I have to eat *noodles?*" and sighed loudly. I said, "Fine," and slammed a pencil and paper down on the table. "Write me a list of *both* things you like." Now I could see the mistakes I had made with Celia, but I was not sure that, given that kind of pressure, I would do any better today.

The year Celia was born, I was sixteen and trying to stop my parents' divorce by not eating and letting my grades nose-dive. Now Celia was sixteen. Her father, Richard, was living in California with an ex–performance artist, Valerie. Her mother, Mona, was a lawyer, now remarried to another lawyer; Celia lived with them outside of Boston. I was living with my husband, Mark, and our one-year-old daughter, Annie, in a condo in Cambridge.

Now Celia was on her way over and I was once again trying to think what to offer her to eat. I didn't have any Coke or potato chips and I wondered whether I had time to scoop up Annie and run to the store. Or would Celia drink Diet Coke now? I decided to skip the Coke and instead made some iced tea the fast way, with a little boiling water and a lot of ice cubes. I hoped the tea wouldn't go cloudy on me as I put on a pair of baggy jeans and a loose white shirt. I worried that these clothes had become dated in the time that I had been distracted by having a baby. In the living room, I opened the sliding glass door to the tiny backyard we shared with our fellow condo owners, brushed some wet leaves off two lawn chairs, and pushed them over next to a tree stump that Mark and I used as a table. I stuck a finger into Annie's diaper: dry. Then I dragged the playpen out of the living room, loaded it with toys, and poured diluted apple juice into a bottle. When the doorbell rang, I went with Annie on my hip, only to notice just before I opened the door that she was suddenly wet and leaking. There was a small dark spot on my pants under her.

Celia looked almost the same, except that she was taller and thinner, her features sharpened slightly. She lifted one hand as if she were about to take an oath and said, "Hello."

I leaned forward to give her a kiss and a one-armed hug, but she didn't reciprocate. "So good to see you," I said. "You look fantastic." I shouldn't have worried about my clothes; I could see that I didn't own anything she would have approved of. She was wearing flowered leggings that came to just below her knees and a hot-pink halter top that showed her stomach, which was flat and tan. Her hair was cut short on one side, sharply outlining her ear, and on the other side swung down to a point that reached her chin. It looked streaked to me, and I caught myself thinking, *At her age?* She was carrying a shopping bag from Urban Outfitters and another from a record store. "Come in," I said. "I can't wait to hear what you've been up to."

"That your kid?" she said.

"Yes. Annie. She's just a year old."

Annie said, "Ba ba?"

"Yes, you'll have an apple-juice ba-ba in just a minute," I said. "I have to change her, Celia, but then maybe you'd like to hold her."

"That's O.K."

"Oh," I said. "Well, why don't you go sit outside. I won't be a minute."

Annie said, "Appa?"

"Yes, apple-juice ba-ba," I said. I changed her diaper and overalls but didn't bother with my own pants. When I came back, Celia was sitting in one of the chairs, rolling Annie's little musical lawn mower back and forth over the dirt next to her foot. I put Annie in the playpen, and mentally thanked her for not screeching in protest. "I made some iced tea," I said. "Would you like some?"

Celia shrugged. "O.K."

I brought it out in tall glasses complete with lemon wedges and some cookies I had been trying not to eat. She took one of these, looked at the top, turned it over, looked at the bottom, and took a bite. Then she sipped her tea. "Do you have any sugar?"

"Right here." I pointed to the sugar bowl.

She put two heaping spoonfuls in her glass, though the tea was already sweetened. Stirring vigorously, she said, "My dad told me you were living here now."

"Did he?" I said. "I'm glad you stopped by." She nodded, unsmiling. Her father and I had split up a few months after Celia visited us in California. That last year before he moved out, every little conflict between us had seemed to take on exaggerated significance for Richard and turned into a major fight. He exploded at me in a supermarket once because he said I always bought the wrong kind of garbage bags—the cheap, too-small kind that slipped down into the can. On my birthday, he gave me diamond earrings, though he knew I didn't like diamonds. After a few days, I asked if I might exchange them for something else that we could pick out together, and he got really angry. So for our anniversary, I decided to wear the earrings as a conciliatory gesture, but by then I couldn't remember where I'd put them for safekeeping. This made him even madder. Instead of going out to dinner as we had planned, he yelled, "You've never liked a single thing I've given you," at me all evening. Finally he threw a teapot at the refrigerator, smashing it into many shards and splinters. That night, Richard packed a couple of suitcases and left. He went to the performance artist's place; they had been seeing each other for quite a while, apparently. When I found that out, the bad year suddenly made a lot more sense.

"Have you seen Richard much lately?" I asked Celia now.

She smirked, raising one side of her mouth in an expression eerily like her father's. "What do you think?"

"Um. No?" I said.

"Bingo," she said. "I haven't been out to California since Valerie had Oscar."

"Oscar?" I said.

"Yeah, Dad and Valerie's kid. He's older than this one, I think." She indicated Annie with a nod of her head.

"Oh," I said.

Celia said, "A few years ago—this was before Oscar—my dad came East to try to get a show on the Cape or in Maine, and my mom made him take me with him when he was making the rounds. We drove to a bunch of tourist places in this rented car. Every morning, he'd drop me at a beach and then take off with his portfolio and slides to galleries. In the evening, he'd pick me up and then we'd eat in some fish place. I got a superb tan." She made an A-O.K. sign with her thumb and forefinger. I wondered whether Richard had made any effort to talk to her, to get her to tell him things, and whether he had given any thought to sunscreen for her. Then I reminded myself that this had nothing to do with me anymore, if it ever had. "I haven't seen my dad since the gallery tour, or since Oscar came on the scene. Take your pick. Sometimes he calls or Valerie sends a birthday present and we all pretend it's from him."

I said, "One good thing about getting older is that things will become easier between you and your parents." She rolled her eyes. I said, "That's what happened to me, anyway." There was a long pause. Celia probably thought I hadn't gotten her point about her father. I tried to think of a way to show her that I had.

Then Celia said, "What's your new husband's name?"

"Mark," I said. "But he's not that new. We've been married two and a half years."

"Whatever," she said. "What's he do?"

"He converts old factory buildings into office space."

"Oh," she said. "Can I see your wedding pictures?"

"Sure," I said, though this was about the last thing I would have expected her to ask. I went to the bedroom bookcase, found our wedding album, and brought it out to her. I said, "Want me to tell you who everyone is?" and leaned forward, prepared to point out certain people and explain how they were related.

"No, that's O.K.," Celia said. She went through the book, page by page, pausing equally at each image. When she was finished, she handed the album back to me without comment. For the next few moments, we both looked at Annie, who said, "Eee," and threw her arms up in the air. I said, "Eee," back and clapped my hands, a new trick Annie had learned to perform on command. She didn't do it this time, though, so I tried again, clapping and saying, "Eee." Nothing. I felt Celia watching me and my face and ears burned.

"She's cute," Celia said.

"Thank you," I said. "I think so, too, but then, I'm her mother." I smiled at Celia, but she wasn't looking at me. There was another silence. "How's school?" I said desperately.

"It's O.K. I didn't go today, though. I came here to shop, instead. I can't take school full time. It gets on my nerves."

"I can understand that."

"Do you have, like, a job or anything?"

"No," I said. "I was working in a gallery on Newbury Street, but I stopped when I had Annie."

"You painting anymore?" she said. I shook my head. "You going to start again?"

"Eventually. But these days I like being with Annie so much that I don't want to do anything else. Honestly, I'm perfectly satisfied staying home." Richard always said that I wasn't focused enough to be an artist; I thought he was right, but I had hoped to force myself to change. "The only problem is that I feel guilty all the time for dropping my work." Now Annie was concentrating hard on banging two plastic cups together. "When she's in school in a couple of years, I'm going to try to paint again." Celia scratched at a spot on her shirt. "Seriously," I said. "I am."

She reached for a cookie. "Mind if I have another? Junk food is one of my weaknesses."

"Have as many as you want."

She took two. "My mother's pregnant, you know. She's due in August."

"How exciting," I said.

"She's forty." Celia took a bite of cookie and chewed thoughtfully. "You'd think she'd have had enough of motherhood after all the crap I've put her through. We get into these intense fights. And like, last year, I stole some money from her and ran away." She checked my face for a reaction. Not wanting to cut her off, I tried not to appear shocked or concerned. "I used her cash card," she said. "The second day, I got caught when I tried to steal some strawberries from a Stop & Shop. Wouldn't you know—the one time I feel like eating something healthy, it gets me in trouble. When the new kid is my age, my mom will be fifty-six. She's lectured me a million times about birth control and a woman's right to decide what happens to her own body, so you have to assume she knows what her options are. It's going to be a boy. She had that test." Celia examined a hangnail. "I don't know," she said. "All these babies."

"I bet it'll be fun having a little brother around," I said. "Think how much you'll be able to teach him from your experience." She rolled her eyes again. We both looked at Annie, who was standing on her xylophone. "Do you do any painting or drawing these days, Celia?" I said. "You used to be very good. We had your pictures all over our kitchen. Remember?"

"I don't remember your house that well," she said. "I was only there a little while. I mostly remember the one with the pool."

She meant the rented house. I'd been thinking about that place, too. During her visit, I had made Richard take Celia to Disneyland by himself so they could spend some time alone together. At the end of the day, I couldn't wait to hear what she had thought of it all. While Richard was putting the car in the garage, I met her at the front door and said, "Well, how was it? Did you go on the Matterhorn? Was Space Mountain open? How about the Pirates of the Caribbean? Did you have a good time?" Celia had glared at me with scalding contempt. She said, "It was Disneyland, O.K.? Big deal. Now would you calm down and leave me alone?" I had gone quietly into our bedroom to look out at the water in the pool and burst into tears in private. Before that visit, I had fantasized that Celia and I would be pals. Foolishly, I neglected to consider that I was not in any position for her to like me.

"How did you meet your husband?" she said now. She picked up the handle of the toy lawn mower again and rolled it around. It tootled an inconclusive little melody.

"See that painting?" I said, pointing into the living room.

"Yeah," she said.

"I sold it to him."

"Oh." Celia looked at her watch. It was black with big white numbers: a quarter after five. "I have to go," she said, standing up.

"That's too bad," I said. "I hope you'll come back again sometime when Mark's home."

As she passed the playpen, Celia said, "So long, little critter." Annie looked up and studied Celia's face for a moment.

Leading the way to the front door, Celia pointed to a copy of *People* lying on a chair. Charles and Di were on the cover again. "Those two hate each other's guts," she said. "I heard that they haven't been in the same room in over two years."

"Oh, I'm sure they don't hate each other," I said. "They just have very different interests."

"Sure," Celia said. "Just keep telling yourself that." At the door, she shrugged and said, "O.K. I just wanted to see, you know, how you turned out." She smirked to let me know that this was a joke.

I said, "Did I turn out all right?" In the silence that followed, I worried that she was going to say something mean and then disappear.

"I guess so," Celia said. "See ya." And she winked.

"Bye," I said. I watched for a minute as she walked down

the street. She pulled a couple of leaves off a lilac bush as she passed, then dropped them onto the sidewalk. I closed the door.

After Celia had gone, I let Annie stumble around in the yard, while I followed to keep her from putting anything really disgusting in her mouth. Then I put her back in her playpen and started gathering the tea things to take inside. I planned the way I would tell Mark the story of Celia's visit. I pictured the two of us, having dinner, after Annie was asleep, theorizing about why Celia had come. Maybe she had always secretly liked me and thought of me today when she wanted to talk to someone. Could Richard have been behind this in some way? I couldn't wait to hear Mark's ideas.

When he arrived, he called out, "Where are the women?" from the living room. He came outside and kissed me first, then he went to the baby. "Hey," he said. "Are you sure you want her playing with this?"

"With what?" I said.

He held up one of those fuzzy gray boxes that jewelry comes in, the corners all wet from Annie's gnawing on it. "Where did she find that?" I said, taking it from Mark. I opened it. Inside were the diamond earrings that Richard had given me for my birthday during the bad year. Celia must have put the box in the playpen when I went in to get the photo album. Was that why she asked to see our wedding pictures? Or had she planted it earlier, when I was getting the tea or changing the baby? It might have happened at the last minute, when she said goodbye to Annie. I pictured Celia as an eleven-year-old, stealing the box from my dresser or wherever it was and taking it home with her. Then a picture of the night Richard left came to mind with a clarity that almost knocked the wind out of me. After the fight about the earrings, I remembered

Richard walking out and slamming the door so hard that it immediately bounced open again. I had stood motionless for a long time after he was gone until I could finally make myself walk across the room to close the door. Then, in a state of panic or shock or despair, I went to the kitchen and crawled around on the floor, sweeping up the pieces of the smashed teapot with my hands. After that night, everything changed for Richard and me. Now I imagined how guilty Celia must have felt keeping the earrings all those years, believing that I wanted and missed them, not knowing the significance they had taken on.

Mark took off his jacket and hung it over the back of the other chair. "It's so nice, why don't we eat out here tonight?" he said. "Where are those bug candles?"

I looked up and said, "What?"

"The bug candles?"

"Oh. Hall closet. Is it chilly out here?" I said. "Do you think Annie should have a sweater?"

"She seems comfortable," Mark said. He picked her up now and started a game they liked to play together, bending way over, his hand supporting the back of her head, making her scream with delight at being upside down.

I said, "I'm going to get her a sweater." In her room, I took out several of Annie's sweaters and rejected each of them in turn. After a few minutes, Mark came in, carrying Annie. "What are you doing in here so long?" he said.

I said, "I can't find what I want." I was looking for some-thing really substantial. What I had in mind, I think, was a sweater that would protect her from everything, including the mistakes I would make as her mother and the miserable, scrap-ing guilt she would experience when, inevitably, she hated me for one thing or another.

Mark took a yellow hooded sweatshirt off the top of the

pile and said, "This is good enough." He stood Annie on the floor and pushed her little soft arms into the sleeves. "Let's go outside," he said to her. She squeaked, and he said, "Yes."

I stayed behind and put all the sweaters back. Then I went to our room and put the earring box in my top drawer underneath a camisole I never wore. I closed the drawer and headed quickly back to the yard.